CW00410522

BRIMSTONE

A fan fiction series set in the universe of
Star Citizen, by Cloud Imperium Games

by

Michael Marks

For Billy
We miss you brother.

Foreward

When I was asked by the popular media site Imperial News Network to produce short stories based on the upcoming game Star Citizen, I leaped at the opportunity. I had long before joined the millions of backers who support what has become the largest crowd-funded project in history, crossing north of $200 million in 2018 and still going strong. It is an audacious project to create a 'game' that, frankly, blurs across the line of a universe simulation. A description of the technologies already achieved would exceed the size of this book.

A fan of sci-fi since childhood, Star Citizen presented an unprecedented palette of colors and textures of life in the far-flung future. It is both breathtaking and gritty, offering an ability to step into the boots of almost any profession, from space pirate to common salvager, to a level of realism never before attempted. It is the game I dreamed of.

The narrative of Brimstone was envisioned in fast-paced, short-format installments. But popular response drove what might have been a short trilogy to become a 233-page novella of sorts. It is presented here in its original format. You don't need to be familiar with the game to enjoy the story, but SC fans have delighted in the many details woven tightly through formal Star Citizen lore. I hope you enjoy it.

FIRE AND BRIMSTONE

LEIR-1 Bravo

They promised they could protect us from anything the Vanduul threw in our direction. That's what governments do; make promises. Pundits were spouting the party line right up to the moment the bomb went off.

That was three years ago. To this day we still aren't sure what the hell it was. We know this much, it wasn't high explosive, it wasn't some amped-up fuel-air device, hell it wasn't even a nuke. Those things we understand. This was something else, something… unnatural. Lacking anything better to offer, the science-geeks coined a name for the device; called it a 'thermoplasmic' weapon.

'*What?*' proved to be only one of the many unanswered questions. '*Why us?*' was a close second. Leir-1 Bravo – second site on the first planet of the Leir System – was just another no-name industrial arcology; a spot-welded sprawl of roughnecks and heavy machines that covered about eighty square kilometers of this barren, un-terraformed planet. No military presence. No agri-base. Hell we were so bad off we had to have breathable atmo shipped in.

What we did have was four working mines; an ant-maze of tunnels and shafts that barfed up a continual stream of strategic metals, graphite and crystals. This in turn fed a chain of refineries, foundries and factories. An outer ring of housing and human amenities wrapped around it all; pretty much a city of airlocks and pressurized hamster-tubes. Still, by any measure we were just one of a number of mining towns in Outsider space; far from the biggest or most prosperous. Any way you looked at it, attacking L1B made no sense.

Living here now means getting used to a lot of shit that doesn't make sense. Like several square kilometers of burned-out ruins that, after three years of non-stop winter, still simmers like a cast-iron stove. No fire, no radiation, just… heat. Figure that one out.

Those ruins used to be City Center. It has different names now; the Nekropolis, O'lik shahar, Urbem mortuorum… but in any language it all means pretty much the same thing. *City of the Dead.* If you've ever walked through the rubble there you'd understand.

For those who haven't seen it, well, the bomb did more than pulverize the Nek, it… changed it; transmogrified steel and flesh like some hellish trick of alchemy. When that searing mass of energy filled the sky, physics came unglued. Solids became un-solid, things blurred into one another before returning a moment later to solids of completely different chemical structure. Today the Nek is filled with wide-eyed corpses that stand like the dead of ancient Pompeii; draugr of asphalt and obsidian.

Most everything in the Nek was fused into a seamless, lava-like crust. A crust, it turns out, that never cools. To this day a greenish steam seeps from cracks in the shell, belching a rotten-egg stench of sulphur laced with the garlic reek of phosporus. It was that hellish smell that finally gave L1B a real name: Brimstone.

Not everyone touched by the fire of that night died. Several thousand outside the Nek were exposed to shades of thermoplasmic hell. You can tell by their scars which way they were facing when it hit. Pebbled textures were branded into flesh. Eyes that gazed on the blast were seared as well, irises charcoaled. Today the blind and the maimed are common in the streets of Brimstone.

As you might guess, there was an immediate rush to get the hell outta Dodge. But with equal speed the UEE slammed a quarantine on transit. Given the immigration crisis playing out all across the Vanduul line, refugees – especially those exposed to some unknown alien event – could not be allowed to scatter among the populated worlds. In back-channel comms that the public media would never hear, UEE politicians, long-chafed by the Outsider government's isolationist stance, told Mya they could take their crisis and shove it. The UEE spent more time setting up blockades at Jump Points than they did trying to help.

The civilian response was only marginally better. Yeah, we became the flavor of the month for a little while, the *cause celebre* that drove the usual crowd of attention-whores to display the blue-purple ribbons, or to flash that pinky-thumb sign of unity that had been used by countless groups beforehand. A StarFund campaign actually crowd-sourced a Freelancer-load of food and clothing that showed up early on. But soon hundreds of charity drives popped up, many proving to be scams or mismanaged debacles that brought little or no relief to ground zero. Like the victims of massive storms in ages past, our story eventually got stale and the news turned its attention to the next compelling disaster. Eight months into our survival, it became pretty clear nobody gave a shit.

Unless you count the Xi'An. Who would have figured that?

Truth be told, I don't think they came to Brimstone expecting to help. It was almost a year after the event that Kray dispatched a token delegation for the sake of public relations, sending some mid-level bureaucrat who lacked the clout to dodge the assignment. They offloaded a shiny little AutoMed and a few conex containers of food, then reluctantly agreed to a brief tour before they shuffled away.

Everything changed when they walked into the Nek.

I couldn't tell you what it was they saw. By all appearance it was just another twisted obelisk of wreckage outside the smoldering maw of Mineshaft 3. But the Xi'An fell on their scaley faces and backed out groveling. Whatever it was, or whatever they think it was, serious help started arriving by the boatload. Building materials, fuel, even three atmo recyclers; everything Brimstone needed get back on its feet, and then some.

Xi'An cruisers started patrolling the borders separating Leir and Vanduul space. That really chapped some UEE ass, especially on occasions when the Xi'An backed up Outsider fleets stationed at the Jump Points.

On a day-to-day basis the Xi'An pretty much keep to theirselves. They don't seem to have any interest in our affairs as long as they have unfettered access to what they've come to call the 'Ménhù' which I guess means holy place or something.

As a result, Brimstone rose from the ashes, a city under no laws but her own. Despite some pointless saber-rattling, the UEE seems reluctant as hell to roll out here with muscle for fear of further galvanizing the Outsiders and the Xi'An. The politics of their own failure made Brimstone something of a steaming turd that the Imperials would rather ignore. That works just fine for us.

Over the next two years a growing body of pirates, smugglers and worse have drifted to our docks, happy for safe haven where ill-gotten gains can be traded without question. Business sprung up catering to that market, places like Roxy's: a one-stop shop for fencing, whoring and gambling. We are not long on doctors in Brimstone, not legit ones anyway, but Mya has a proper hospital if somebody needs major re-assembly.
The Banu are underfoot pretty much all the time. Those fuckers would sell their grandma if she'd fetch a good price. Without a blink they took to Brimstone as any other underserved market. A lot of stolen cargo filters back into the rest of the 'verse on Banu ships.

Despite our wayward ways and all the bad blood, we still do some business with the Empire. They have a ravenous appetite for strategic metals, even if those deals are normally worked through brokers of dubious repute that have no traceback to respectable firms. It turns out that once you get past all the posturing, nothing in the 'verse is really wrong as long as it makes a profit.

Brimstone has become a place where a lot of people live, where a fair few of them die, a place where concepts like rights and law don't survive a meter past your ability to enforce 'em. It is a maze of cold, dark alleys and underground tunnels where we look askance at *pinks*, unblemished off-worlders who don't carry the scars of that night. At its center, Brimstone is a graveyard where the dead never fell to the ground, where ghosts and aliens roam through the ashes together.

This is Brimstone: an armpit of industry, a criminal haven, the last outpost on the edge of nothing. And these are her stories.

I MAKE IT A SEVEN

Elysium Sector
Idris-M Frigate *SS James Archer*
The Command Deck

"She's running sir."

Captain Ron Scanlon shook his head. Pinging an active scan is like turning on the light in the galley; the cockroaches always panic. He closed his eyes and made a tired, back-handed gesture towards the main screen. "Explain it to her, Lieutenant."

"Aye sir."

Scanlon knew from the sudden THRUM that a beam of crimson energy just lanced out from an overhead turret, cutting a brilliant line through the darkness of space. Knowing Colter's flair for the dramatic, the shot probably scorched paint off the nose of the Freelancer.

"She's shutting down sir. Engines off, shields off, lights on."

"Uh huh." Scanlon sighed as he opened his eyes. *Funny how that works.* He glanced over at Colter. "What do you think? A Six?"

Colter gave the question a moment of serious thought. "Well he did try to run sir, and this is a Tier-One zone. I make it a Seven."

Scanlon narrowed his eyes. "You're a hard man Colter."

A grin creased the younger man's face. "Just doing my part to keep the system safe sir." The delivery was almost believable.

Scanlon stood up and tossed the ComTab into Colter's lap. "Lemme know what you find." He couldn't help but chuckle as he walked off the bridge.

Navy doctrine had protocols for everything, and by the book, all interdictions were to be treated alike. That's not how things worked out here in the black. There wasn't enough time to run a down-to-the-bolts check on every two-bit hauler that may or may not be smuggling crap across the galaxy. Scanlon was here to guard against the Vanduul, who lurked *en masse* just a single jump away. When every search is a 10, your inspection teams get numb. They get sloppy.

The flip side of that coin was every bit as important; the unspoken understanding between hunters and hunted. Don't run; don't make me chase you. Shut down, play nice, we do a casual glance for VBT, Very Bad Things, and everybody goes on their merry way.

If you run, you lie, or God help you, if you point so much as a sharp stick at one of my men, things will go very differently.

'Different' covered a very wide range. Border duty on the fringe might feel like a career dead-end, but it has its perks, autonomy being one of them. Scanlon could order a ship dismantled down to her floorplates, even call in a Crucible to do the job right. If really pissed off, a Border Patrol Captain could have a suspect ship fed to a Reclaimer, one of those big flying shredders, "just to be on the safe side."

That last option could put solid cash into the pocket of a savvy Captain. Vulture Teams hung around for just that purpose, listening to police-band comms on the hope that a six-hundred metric ton metal-grinder might prove handy.

Hence the 10-scale. If a response gets above a Five, things start getting broken. At Eight, somebody's getting hurt. Tens are easy; a Ten never happened. When you shove a boat deadstick into a star's gravity well, there's no need to write a report.

Things only work out here when everybody understands the rules.

"You just don't understand the fucking rules, do you?" Scanlon slapped the tablet down on the steel table. The little counter in the back of his mind had already climbed to an 8.

"What's to understand?" Rayson Drax held up his hands. "I'm a businessman. I thought you guys were pirates. What can I say? I panicked."

Judging by the calm he showed in his current predicament, Scanlon guessed that Drax wasn't prone to panic. The natty man in the leather coat leaned back, projecting thinly veiled condescension.

"Look Cap, this is going nowhere. You ain't found anything on my boat because there's nothing to find."

"Nothing besides the dead body?"

Drax face-palmed, venting his own growing frustration. "How many times I gotta tell you? The stiff was a floater. I got the tag, stuck him in the hold and out of the goodness of my heart I'm taking him home to…"

Scanlon glared as Drax ran on. The story on the corpse was likely true; it had been dead for a while, a freeze-dried floater with no sign of foul play. The cursory Medscan said that the tumor in its brain was a more likely COD than some lead pipe to the skull. With some of these roughneck outfits, a poor bastard dying in his sleep is just as likely to get spaced out the airlock. One less share of the profits to haggle about with the widow. Still, the fact that any part of Drax's story might be legit pissed Scanlon off even more.

"Do you think I'm stupid?" Scanlon growled.

Drax might have been tempted to reply, but wisely shut up.

Scanlon placed his fingertips on the tablet and rotated it slowly to face the manacled prisoner. Most of the gloss surface was taken up by a rap sheet that carried numerous jurisdictional icons.

"You have outstanding warrants in four UEE sectors. The Xi'An want you for questioning, you are travelling under a forged Banu registration, you've even pissed off the Outsiders."

Drax twitched. Tiny, just a hint of stiffness. Eyes flicked down and left.

"What, you thought I wouldn't find out that the Leirans have, what, a hundred grand on your head? Looks like that natural charm of yours isn't working anywhere."

Drax tried to glare back but his veneer began to fray. "Look, you don't work for those wackjobs, you're UEE. So take me to Idris, Centauri, wherever —"

Scanlon chuckled, the sound laced with sneer. "Idris? Centauri? Places where, remarkably enough, you have no criminal record at all. Places where scumbag lawyers working for whatever syndicate you're in are just waiting to sweep this away with an envelope of cash to a crooked Magistrate."

Scanlon's eyes narrowed, shifting from the tablet to Drax. A smile tugged at the Captain's lip as he saw a faint sheen on the criminal's brow. "You're sweating."

Drax swallowed. "We can work something out."

"With what? A corpse-sicle and a hold full of salvage? You don't bring much to the table."

"Look Cap, be reasonable—"

Scanlon placed his hands on the cold steel and leaned forward, coming nose-to-nose with Drax. His voice was now a Nine-Plus snarl. "You had your chance to be reasonable, to follow the rules. But you thought it would be funny to jerk me around. That's not how things work. So let's see how funny the Outsiders find it."

Drax swallowed hard. "You wouldn't."

A shudder went through the floor as docking clamps released and the two huge bodies separated. While no sound carried in space, it was a sure bet that the UEE boat was already engines-hot, double-timing it back for the Elysium Jump Point. Back to home space. The mil-ship had all the badges it needed to get into Leiran space, but getting back out might not be so easy. That too, is how things worked.

Drax leaned against the pile of cargo MagLocked to the floor. A broad smirk creased his face as he looked up at the camera. With a cocksure flourish he swept both hands towards the stack. "Ta-daaa."

The overhead beacon still rotated red, claxon blaring. It was the normal process as a computer in the ceiling made sure that both doors were sealed before opening either one.

The smuggler wiped a soiled sleeve across his face, dragging a clotted smear of red from his beard. It was hardly the worst beating the feds had ever thrown him, but it's never fun to play the punching bag. Still, he was sure they'd hold back; you don't get paid on a 'Deliver Alive' bounty if the subject is dead. Drax had been real specific on that point when he arranged for the bounty in the first place.

A hard metal bang resonated through the floor as pneumatic rams drew back the door-bolts. The beacon flashed to yellow and, thankfully, the claxon ceased its blaring. The heavy inner door rose ponderously into the ceiling. Drax' smile grew when he saw the grey-clad figure standing back-lit in the cloud of vapor.

"And you said there was no way to get through the UEE blockade." Drax stepped forward with a swagger. "Oh ye of little faith…"

He stopped in his tracks as six figures appeared to flank the Man in Grey. Guys in armor. Half a dozen ARs snapped up like switchblades.

"Hey woah, woah!" Drax backpedaled, open hands reflexing up in plain sight. The confusion on his face gave way to concern, this time the genuine article. "Dude, it's there, it's all there. Every scrap."

A team of four technicians scuttled into the chamber; the six guns didn't flinch. Drax watched as the yellow-suits powered off the MagLocks and started moving containers; tossing electronic components aside with hurried disdain. They paused at the long metal box.

"That's just the stiff," Drax muttered. "The hard drives are over there. I mean, I figure that's what this is all about." Drax looked up at Grey, trying to get some sort of engagement. "Nice touch with the dead guy though, lotta plausible deniability with that one. I gotta remember that in the fu–"

Drax' words were cut off by the high-pitched whine of a laser-saw, and the sudden smell of burning flesh as the head was expertly severed. The tech team lifted it from the makeshift coffin and placed it into a small, cylindric cryotank. When the latch hissed shut, they turned and marched briskly out between the picket line of armor.

A loud bang overhead and the claxon blared anew as the beacon switched back to red. With a groan the inner door began to close. Six muzzles adjusted as Drax took a panicked step forward. No click of safeties coming off, no movie bullshit of bolts-slamming-forward as if they'd been on open chambers. If there was any sound that one might have heard over the deafening noise, it would have been the faint creak of slack coming out of well-oiled triggers. That and the sudden, fabric-tearing pucker of Drax's ass.

As the inner door slammed shut, Drax could hear screaming. He realized it was his own just before the outer door blew open with the whoosh of a passing jet. The last thing Drax knew was a cold, infinite silence.

GNAWING ON THE BONES

Caliban Sector
Aegis Reclaimer *Goliath*

"Debris out." Tank's voice – just a whisper on the comm – was clear in the still, frigid air.

My breath fogged in the dark cabin as I watched pieces of wreckage drift away from the ship. I made out the silhouette of a turbofan engine, a burned-out APU, a cryogenic tank; those just a handful of the couple dozen hunks of scrap that Tank shoved out the forward airlock.

The trick was hardly original. Wiley submarine captains back in World War II would eject anything that floats – oil, cushions, even dead bodies – out through torpedo tubes in an effort to appear dead in the water.

There's no water out here in deep space, but the Caliban Ring was long on wreckage; more than anyone could scan all at once. It was the biggest hide-n-seek field in the galaxy. Until you knew what might be lurking in the shadows, it was better to look like just another gutted hulk drifting through the black.

Doing so meant freezing your ass off in damn-near full shut down; engines, lights all off, even life support at bare minimum. By design, tiny random signatures emanated from some of the scrap we set adrift; things like intermittent arcs and radio static that added to the haze of electromagnetic white noise permeating deep space. From solar winds to distant broadcasts and gravitic anomalies, there is more sensor-blurring shit than you might imagine in the middle of nothing.

For the last ninety minutes *Goliath* had tumbled a crawling, end-over-end course that I hoped would look happenstance when it was anything but. Pulling off a dead-stick drift to a precise point in space – especially through a lot of floating wreckage – took skill, planning and a bucket full of balls. As beefy as *Goliath* was, getting crunched between a couple of stadium-sized hulls could kill you just as dead as enemy lasers.

Stretching almost a hundred-sixty meters from nose to stern, this Aegis Reclaimer was every bit the behemoth her name implied, an industrial-grade beast that towered over a normal collection of vessels. But the ships that formed the Caliban Ring were anything but normal. The war that raged here back in '71 was a slugfest that left an armada of dead capitol ships in a sea of lesser vessels; corvettes, frigates and fighters. A tangled web of human and Vanduul bodies and technology. Out here, *Goliath* could well be just another over-stuffed coffin that long ago cooled to ambient temperature. That was the plan anyway.

Salvagers, people like me, had been coming out to the Ring for years, picking at the bones of these dead leviathans. Yeah, you could argue we serve an important role, cleaning up messes and recycling materials to make shiny new stuff. But the harsh truth is that we're really a bunch of adrenaline-fueled gambling addicts, treasure hunters looking to find the next Holy Grail floating out here in the black. The next run, we tell ourselves, is gonna be the Big One. That dream is our crack cocaine.

Polite society, people not like me, frown on pillaging the Ring. Most of them view the endless stretch of corpse-littered wrecks as some sort of giant graveyard, sanctified by the thousands of lives snuffed out in that horrific dance of laser beams and missile trails. That's a noble thought, the kind of tear-inducing sentiment you find on a Hallmark card. Sadly, it's a bunch of baloney. Not one of the crusty corpse-sicles floating wide-eyed in the cold can do a damn thing with the wealth of metal around them. The ghosts of this place won't rest any easier if I turn around and go home, and they sure as hell wouldn't pay my bills when I got there. A good reactor core on the other hand…

That was the real trick of making money in this business. 'Struct' is your basic scrap, structural hull beams rich with stuff like chromium and titanium alloys. That's what ships are made of and it can be harvested in abundance out here. Decent value-to-weight ratio, but it takes hard work and puts a helluva lot of expensive wear and tear on the grinders in *Goliath's* belly that chew 40-mil I-beams into storable scrap.

If you were willing to spend some EVA time with a plasma torch in hand you could scour the war-hammered wrecks and cherry-pick things like undamaged graphene armor plates. Specialty items like weapons and armor, especially ones you can't buy on the civilian market, pull big bucks from mechanics who service the 'merc and pirate communities.

For the really stout-hearted salvors, digging deeper into a wreck might produce all sorts of treasure. A crate of Latinum bars maybe, or an undamaged arc reactor. You might tumble to a memory core that still holds information long thought lost; we're talking scrap of an altogether different nature but it could prove invaluable to the right customer. Or to that customer's biggest competitor. Admittedly, it could also get you killed, but every job has its downsides.

For a lot of salvors, the payoff for a cargo-hold jammed full of 'struct' didn't balance up against the risks of farming the Ring. Things prowled these wrecks, things that came from human and Vanduul space alike. Anywhere you find sailors you will find old stories, gloomy tales that hang like cigar smoke in dank, dockyard bars. Tales of crews that slid into madness and cannibalism, of ghost ships or modern-day sea serpents. Terrible fanged things that hunted salvagers, explorers and historians alike. Millennia after man feared sailing off the edge of a flat world, sailors still love to tremble at things that go bump in the night.

I've seen some weird shit in my day and trust me, I don't laugh no matter how crazy the story. That's bad luck. But the biggest hazard I figure I'm likely to run into is the law, or someone just like me looking to break it. Those guys run the gamut from pirates or vigilantes to zealot fanatics standing holy watch over the honored dead. Whatever their motive, most of the things you were likely to encounter out here had a vested interest in leaving no witnesses.

That last point was no small matter. In normal space, in normal times, it was still considered 'good form' to rescue a stranded sailor be he friend or foe, partner or rival, captain and crew alike. If you find somebody floating in one of those damn insulated coffins of an escape pod, you drag 'em in, patch their hurt and haul 'em somewhere safe, even if just to dump their ass on some back-water station where they could cool their heels for weeks, maybe months, to catch a ride home. But you don't abandon someone to slowly die all alone in the dark.

It was an unspoken code, an honor thing, a professional courtesy if you will, that underneath it all recognized a simple fact of life. Space is a big empty place and the guy you save today might tomorrow be looking out his windshield at your escape pod. Word gets around and a positive balance in the Bank of Karma wasn't a bad thing to have.

The Ring had more bad karma than it had wrecks. Out here were guys who would blow an escape pod out of the sky for laughs, or haul it onboard just to look the occupant in the eye as they put a bullet through his melon. Some would do a whole lot worse.

"Jesse?" My question didn't need the comm; my co-pilot sat in the seat next to mine. I couldn't see her eyes, hidden behind the sleek VR headset that allowed her to watch a low-power screen with no visible light leaking into the cabin.

"Waypoint in six hundred thirty meters. Closing at 4 per sec." Jesse was all business when the game was on, her normally fiery humor muted to the essentials. At the moment she was the only person onboard who had big eyes on the area around us, although limited to data gathered from passive sensors dotted along *Goliath's* hull. But if something out there had a signature, be it EM or thermal, she should be able to see it. 'Should' being the pivotal word.

Sensing my question, as she usually did, she added "Looks quiet."

It always does, I groused inwardly, right up to the point it gets loud. Prosthetic fingers stroked my chin, the silicone skin of my left hand rubbing the scar that ran the line of my jaw. This wasn't my first rodeo and I knew just how fast an 'easy money' run could go all to shit.

But Welker knew better than to fuck me, I told myself for the hundredth time. He damn well knows I'd kill him if he did. That meant only one of two things; either his info was legit or Welker was certain that whatever was out here would kill me first. Either way, he ends up with a clean slate and me off his list of creditors.

A cynical mix of common sense and experience told me which answer was probably the right one, but damn, if there was even a slim chance…

"Four hundred meters."

Only a few more seconds to make the call. We could play it safe, float by and spend the next hour or two drifting away as quietly as we arrived. Maybe unseen, maybe not. Or we tap the brakes, come to a stop and fire up the lights. If the Reaper was really there we'd see it, just like anything within a few thousand kilometers would know we were here as well.

My mind crunched the numbers. Seconds to target: twenty. Probability that a two-bit skel like Welker would get his hands on good digits about the location of a wrecked Reaper: damn near zero. Value of a Reaper's engine, weapon control panel, shield box, hell just about any intact system… A sigh slipped from my lips. That is a big-ass number.

"Waypoint in five, four…" Jesse's voice ticked the countdown like a machine.

My eyes swept the darkness. Nothing outside but twisted hulls drifting against the black of night.

"Three, two…"

No guts, no glory. I leaned forward in my chair and said "All stop."

Half a dozen thrusters around *Goliath's* hull flared to life. Our lazy tumble shuddered to a halt and the jets just as quickly shut off. Maybe two seconds at the most, so quick you might miss it if you blinked. But things hiding in the dark didn't blink.

If it's out there, I thought, we just sent up a flare. No point in being cagey now.

"Light 'er up."

Rows of external floodlights blazed to life, along with our engines and internal systems. At this point we needed to be operational as quickly as possible. Air, stale but comparatively warm, belched out of the overhead vents. The screens in front of me flickered, pixels resolving into data and imagery that scrolled at a feverish pace. My gaze fell on one display where a blue incremented ring labeled SHIELD built one glowing brick at a time.

Some two thousand meters off our nose the white light splashed across the side of a gutted Bengal. My right hand, the one made of meat and bone instead of carbon fiber and flexinol, swung a gimballed spotlight from left to right. The carrier's outer hull was pock-marked with countless holes burned into armor plate. One of her hangar bays gaped like an open clamshell, onion-layers of I-beam and metal skin peeled back by a massive internal explosion. In the darkness within I could see the chewed-up remains of Avengers plastered along the hangar walls.

A slow whistle slid across my lips; the old girl had taken one hell of a beating before giving up the ghost.

It was what I didn't see that worried me; the ass-end of a Reaper. According to Welker's story, some drug cartel mule running a Hull-C full of Hex had to play duck-and-cover when another vessel passed within sensor range. The mule hunkered up against the belly of a dead Bengal they said, a Bengal at this location. That's when they supposedly saw the wing; angular sawtooth profile, forty, maybe fifty meters in length. Definitely Vanduul, but way too big to be a Scythe. The alien ship looked to have pancaked into the Bengal's hull, fucked its nose all to hell in the process, but the ass end – the engine end – was unbroken.

Like most drug-dealing scum who stumble into more dumb luck than they deserve, the mule ostensibly made it back unscathed, its crew drawn like moths to whatever skel bar they called home. There one guy tells another guy until the story falls into the lap of a crudball like Welker, who owes me… owes me big. He figures a lead like this might square his tab.

A grimace tugged at my face. There were thirty ways the story reeked of bullshit. But what if…?

I took another glance at the screen; our shield was pushing up across forty percent. Safety said wait but time was short and ticking fast. I needed to put eyes on the Bengal's belly.

"Down ninety."

Thrusters along the top of our hull blazed and *Goliath* sank, spotlights wheeling up to smear white ovals across the massive carrier's ruptured gut. My eyes scoured the expanse of grey steel, trying to pick out anything, even the hint of anything, that looked remotely Vanduul. But there was no wing, no angular fuselage. I knew Welker had fucked us even before I saw the Cutlass.

The grey-black ship spun up fast, racks of ambush capacitors flushing life-giving power into her systems in the blink of an eye. She wouldn't have shields for a few moments; there's a limit to what can be done to shove those power-hogs any faster. Tiny by comparison, she'd certainly be up-armored and over-gunned; something kinetic that didn't need a lot of juice to fire. True to stereotype she came out blazing. No monologue, no demands. These guys were pros.

Their gunner was as accurate as he was decisive. The heavy twin-turret perched on the Cutlass' spine belched a jagged line of shells across the face of our ship. Raufoss rounds by the flash of impact; armor-piercing incendiary. Mil-spec. Rounds like that can chew through the hull of frigate, but *Goliath* wasn't some factory-grade Reclaimer. I shoved the stick to one side, slewing our nose off the Cutlass' line of fire. We were tough, but we weren't invulnerable.

The Cutlass slid to hold its point of aim and a white starburst splayed across the front window. Sonofabitch was aiming at us, personally, not looking to kill an engine or powerplant so we could have a polite conversation. A quick glance told me our shield spin-up had reached eighty-seven percent. I barked, "Jesse?"

Despite the cannon-fire blazing outside the window, her eyes were glued to the display, fingers dancing madly. She shouted over the din of one-sided battle. "Two-forty starboard, three hundred gets us overlap."

I keyed the docking thrusters to full and stomped the auxiliaries. *Goliath* abruptly rolled right, the ball-peen hammering outside the flight deck smearing down our port side, meandering from our nose to the angular belly framed by our engine nacelles.

If you've never seen a Reclaimer take off, it's a helluva sight. Those engines vomit an F5 tornado of flame that can deadlift half a million tons of ship and cargo. As *Goliath* rolled onto her right shoulder, those engines swung up. The Cutlass got a facefull of nozzle as we opened the barn doors to hell.

Scumbag or not, I had to give their pilot points for reaction speed. The Cutlass lurched to her port, bursting from our thrust column in a howling powerslide of flame and blistered reflec. Her starboard forewing was burned away, edges of the severed stump glowing incandescent orange. Further aft, her entire starboard engine was charred and misshapen. Whispy tendrils of fire stretched out from her innards, writhing into the vacuum of space.

The evasion carried the Cutlass the better part of three hundred meters to our starboard. Maybe more, maybe less. Good enough. A last glance confirmed our shield ring burned full. Both fists gripped my chair as I growled through clenched teeth, "Hit it."

Jesse's finger stabbed down on the panel and a coded signal pulsed out, tripping passive sensors in each of twenty-some-odd pieces of debris we had scattered through the area. The warheads buried inside them had been cannibalized from the kind of ordinance you find out here, Marksmen, Stalkers, an old Mark IV torpedo. Nothing sexy, just backyard engineering really, but the Cutlass was within the frag radius of three. One of them floated less than a hundred meters above her top-turret. They all detonated.

There's no shockwave in space, no atmo to carry the hull-bursting force of compression that ages ago broke the spine of sea-going vessels. Our shields soaked up what few bits of white-hot frag sizzled in our direction.

The Cutlass wasn't so lucky. When the flash cleared the pirate slid into a slow yaw, venting high-pressure gas from half a dozen holes punched through her hull. Whatever breathable air she contained was hemorrhaging rapidly out into space. The heavy turret was shredded, the gunner reduced to bits of organic splatter.

I looked through our scarred window and zoomed in on the pilot, his cockpit thick with smoke. He yanked frantically at a blaze yellow seat-handle that refused to budge. Judging from the blood spray inside the canopy, whatever punched through the ejector must have caught a piece of him as well.

Goliath edged forward, coming almost nose-to-nose as spider-web fractures fanned across the pirate's canopy. With a busted ejector, the man inside didn't have much time. With a whine of hydraulics, *Goliath* reached out with her huge metal arm.

The pilot and I stared at each other across the airless gap, both of us knowing that I could grab his entire ship and bring it safely into our hold. That's what civilized people did.

But we both knew that was never going to happen. Karma cuts both ways.

Goliath's massive fist closed and his cockpit crumpled in a cloud of vapor and shattered plexi.

A SECOND HEAD

Brimstone
Eastside Industrial Quad

"A second head? Like, what… a mutant?"

"No, like a guy dat brought a spare. C'mon Doc, Boss's waitin." Gort laid a beefy hand on my shoulder, steering me towards the door when I tried to turn back for my jacket. "You won't be needin' dat."

I felt my stomach sink. "Tell me it isn't in the Nek."

Gort shrugged, his thick features scrunching like they usually do when he tries to think. "Not so much in the Nek as right up against it. But plenty warm." He patted me firmly on the back, a gesture I took to be half-reassurance, half-propulsion. Gort wasn't a bad guy, but standing well over two meters tall and a hundred-eighty kilos, with an IQ on par with his shoe size, he wasn't a guy to challenge if you didn't have to. Or if you didn't have a bazooka.

We plodded through a series of airlocks, some of which were propped open. We had the Xi'An to thank for that, those new domes covering sections of town where the atmo recyclers churned out breathable air. Even with the sulfur smell it was better than life in an oversized habitrail.

We cut left, Gort nudging me along an elevated walkway over one of the more intact corners of the Nek. I could feel the heat rising from the blackened structure below. It had been a Revel & York pre-fab center, turning out modular steel frameworks that would get bolted together on-site to become some rich guy's high-end hangar.

Half a dozen roughnecks were in the yard when it happened; three got melted into a T-beam they were lifting, another one sat fused into the seat of a forklift. I knew two of them by name. A shiver ran up my spine as I looked down, as if the silent figures were looking back.

Tired of pushing, Gort passed me by and led the way down a staircase to a cavernous factory bay. I blinked rapidly as we entered, trying to adjust to the bright lights that had been parked around the workshop floor. Most of the beams were aimed at a body sprawled on the concrete floor. A body which, thankfully, had but one head and that in rather unremarkable configuration. Well, aside from the smoking hole where a left eye had been.

I threw Gort a hurried glance wrapped in a shrug of confusion. He rolled his eyes towards the workbench where what was left of another human head hung in some sort of stainless steel halo apparatus.

I grimaced. *Well, now it all makes sense.*

'So whadda ya think?" Like Gort, Lazlo had the local Brimstone way with language, an inarticulate pattern akin to talking with a mouth full of gravel. But Lazlo was no average street-mutt hired for the muscle in his arms. Lazlo was the Alpha Street Mutt, a beast of dubious breeding who, despite his smaller stature, had a bite that kept the bigger dogs in line. From extortion to bookies and drugs, even dogfights, if it ran in Eastside, Lazlo had a toe in it.

I ruffled fingers through my hair, wishing I had grabbed for coffee instead of my jacket. Patting my pockets for a stim to flush the residual haze out of my brain it struck me, *'I've been vertical for six minutes, here for six seconds, and you want to know what I think?'*

"Who's the stiff?" I asked instead, hoping to fill in some of the bigger blanks while I pulled my shit together.

"Some pink," Lazlo spat the word. "Traveling on diplomatic creds. Hit planetside a couple weeks ago, looks like somebody kept him under wraps until yesterday afternoon. That's when a factory security guy hears shots, comes gallopin' to find this."

I circled the body, noting details. Dead guy's white labcoat was pocked with two circular burnmarks. No blood, so whatever did it self-cauterized. The gear on the workbench would have been shiny new as well, had the various components not been equally riddled. Neat round holes lipped in bubbled black. Even in the Brimstone air I could pick out the smell of fresh-burned plexan. Definitely not a slug gun; a beamer of some kind.

"OK, this guy," I muttered with a nod to the corpse, "was running some kinda… science experiment on…" my hand waved off in the direction of the head as I struggled against a wave of hangover nausea.

Lazlo snorted, turning to his assembled thugs with a derisive laugh. "For this bit of brilliance I need a Doc?"

I'm not a Doc– I choked back the words before they came off my lips, that argument long since past and lost. Flushed out of residency with two dead interns on my permanent record, I couldn't get a job as a prison nurse back home, much less as a doctor. But out here, snatch one flatliner back from the dead in a back alley and everybody acts like you're God. Well, it helps if it's the right flatliner.

So now Lazlo thinks I'm the brain surgeon, the coroner, the crime scene investigator. The guy who can just look at things and 'do science shit' to pull answers out of thin air. Reality doesn't much matter, Lazlo isn't a guy to disappoint and I sure as shit don't wanna be the guy to do it.

I patted down my pockets, cursed, then reached blindly towards Gort with a 'gimme' gesture. He pulled a smoke from his pocket, lit it up and handed it over. I sucked in a lungful of Tevarin Green, blinking hard as the first dazzle swept across my vision. Then clarity hit me like sinuses opening. The cobwebs burned away and I took a second deep breath, pacing now, focusing on the fine print.

Might as well start with the head on the workbench.

"Ok, this guy saw some hard miles." Aside from the obvious –the whole decapitation thing – the head itself seemed largely free of mortal trauma. No GSW, no caved-in skull. The skin had that freeze-dried texture that bodies get after a long time in space. The stainless steel halo supported three scan bars equally spread around the mummified melon.

I looked at the severed neck; a perfect cut. "This…" I pointed at the neck, then made a slashing motion across my own, "this happened last, long after he was frozen."

But why cut a head off a frozen corpse?

I chewed on the question. A head has gotta be the most identifiable part; if you were able to ditch the rest, why not send it all to the same fate? Unless you needed to demonstrate to somebody that the guy was dead. Maybe this is a trophy. But that wouldn't need all this other shit, not unless…

I turned back to the parade of gear and dataprints scattered down the workbench. Until they'd been shot all to hell this had been top-notch shit. Bioscanner, biopsy station, DNA sequencers, spectrograph, hell some gizmos I didn't recognize at all. Half a dozen screens hung askew on an articulated rack.

I pulled out my phone and pointed it at the central screen, then punched the monitor's power button. For just a heartbeat the panel flickered, stuttered, sparked violently and settled back to dead.

Lazlo squinted at me, watching closely as I tapped the video app into playback, frame-by-frame. At 12K rez the phone could only grab a few hundred frames per second, but that was enough to catch the fleeting ghost of the last image still caught in hardware. Despite some breakup from a bit of bad interlacing, the image looked like a 3D scan of a brain, with an ugly-ass tumor spidered through the frontal lobe.

"See," Lazlo said to his guard dogs with obvious pride. "Science shit."

He might have been impressed, but as I glanced back at the body on the floor, I was more confused than ever.

What the fuck were you thinking, I silently asked the dead guy, not expecting a reply. But the question was a valid one; when somebody hands you a frozen severed head, it's a little late for oncology.

My eyes narrowed, mental gears grinding against one another. Presuming the dead guy wasn't some wandering, over-equipped idiot with a head fetish, what the hell was he up to? I slid my gaze down the assembly line. What would someone be doing… sequencing the DNA… of an old frozen tumor?

I peered at the device at the end of the line, a dark, olive-grey box largely devoid of interface. Unlike the blue-white hues of lab gear, this thing had a ruggedized military vibe. I spun it around, looking for some sort of manufacturer's ID plate. My eyes fell on a narrow strip: Origin Cryptosystems, a division of Origin Inc.

Crypto? Some kinda code?

I picked up a crumpled datasheet and saw what looked to be a breakdown of DNA. It had the usual suspects, cytosine, guanine, even a couple of the new DNA components we'd come to find in the alien races. But I noticed other stuff, chemical components that had no place in living tissue, malignant or otherwise. I picked up a second page, a third, then turned to look at the head.

The mass behind that withered forehead hadn't grown, it was engineered; built at a molecular level to hide a message that would pass any known scan. The volume of data you could bury in a DNA construct was… shit, it was staggering! Hundreds of terabytes, maybe thousands. I turned right, my gaze returning to the decryption gear. Military decryption. Unless I missed my guess, the DNA in that tumor was a blueprint all right, but not for something living.

A secret somebody was willing to go to a lot of trouble to conceal.

YO-HO YO-HO, A PIRATE'S LIFE FOR ME

Deep Space - Garron System

Dallas paced in the frigid Cutlass, flexing the carbon nanotube muscles in his right fist. He looked out the open back door, MobiGlas scanning the infinite night for the nine other ships that, like the *Ranger*, coasted engines-off through the black. Not one bracket flashed up in his augmented vision, a fact that drew a wicked grin. The other sharks hurtling in formation were as near-frozen as the ship in which Dallas, and the pirates around him, now rode.

He looked around the hold at men and women, all bristling with guns and blades. Like Dallas, most had at least one replacement part fused into their flesh; a hand, a foot, patches of simskin covering artificial teeth. Catastrophic wear and tear was an integral part of this line of work.

Bulldog popped the powercell from his Arclight, rubbed the contacts against his trouser leg and slapped the unit back into the base of the gun. Dallas nodded when their eyes briefly met; a mutual affirmation of readiness and bloodlust. They could taste the fight.

Dallas was old school, a slug man. The LH-86 was slung low on his right thigh like an old west gunslinger. He was good with the pistol, but the only job of a handgun was to get you to a long gun. The Kastak strapped across his back was a deck-cleaner, an electric-driven shotgun that could fill a corridor with meat-chewing flechettes. The extra mag of FRAG-8s were for bigger game; high explosive rounds that could kill a forklift.

He walked to the front of the hold, passing under Gordo in the top turret. Dallas opened the cockpit door and Keller looked back from the RIO seat as Dallas shrugged. The second-seater glanced at his HUD, then rocked back flashing five, then four fingers. Dallas nodded and closed the door, turning back aft.

Every eye in the hold, real and artificial alike, watched him with a hunger. He flashed five-zero, accounting for the four seconds that ticked away. Bolts slammed forward a final time, bodies bracing against weapon racks and cargo nets. Everybody turned their attention towards the open rear door.

The plan was a violent one, and it would happen fast. Gliding in cold they should be on top of the *Co'Ral*, a Banu Merchantman, before it saw them coming. With luck they'd get in a free volley from stealth.

The commercial hauler was no pushover, and its response would be fast and furious. The ragtag collection of Cutlass, Hornets and Avengers would have to dodge a lot of fire while power-sliding, ass-doors open, slinging EVA-suited boarders down the length of the *Co'Ral*. If they were lucky, really lucky, they'd have five or six seconds before every gun on the Banu boat was locked on a target.

That was the hope anyway, because if they failed to draw the *Co'Ral's* suppressive fire, the Warlock would be a sitting duck. Like the sharks, the EMP ship was coming in cold, but from the opposite direction. Unlike the black-coated predators that could shoot from the cover of darkness, the Warlock would have to light up like a pinball machine before pulling the trigger on its weapon. Not a gun, not a torpedo, but a magnetic pulse that could knock a ship's electronics silly without blowing holes through the hull.

Holes are bad; cargo gets sucked out through holes. Put enough holes in a ship and it comes apart altogether. That doesn't make for a profitable run.

The *Ranger's* wall-displays flared to life and Dallas felt the sideways shove of the thrusters. *Game on.*

The tail of the Cutlass went into a sick yaw, the wide expanse of the *Co'Ral* sliding into view. Dallas took one step towards the rear door when an explosion tore through the ceiling, spraying chunks of Gordo and turret-gun across the hold.

Pirates bounced in every direction as the *Ranger* tumbled from the impact. A burst of Banu CIWS chewed the boat, punching hundreds of narrow-spaced holes down the length of the fuselage. Braxton came apart in a spray of crimson. A leg bounced off the ceiling, it might'a been Vickers'. Adrenaline surging, Dallas shouldered past Bulldog and threw himself through the door.

From the sudden openness of space the *Co'Ral* looked like a wall of gunfire. Muzzle flash burned from far more turrets than a merchantman had any business packing. Just a couple hundred meters away, the *Red Revenge* took a square hit to the cockpit, hull-metal peeling back like a titanium banana.

Dallas tumbled away from the *Ranger*, firing suit-jets madly to stabilize his flight. Around him was the black of space, the orange-over-grey of gunfire across the immense starship…

and a dazzling blue. A ball of cyan so bright it threatened to overload his Mobi. Lightning crackled from the center of the glow, then everything went white as the Warlock pulsed.

"Muh-ther-fucker," Dallas cursed furiously, trying to blink away the spots that burned across his vision.

EMP fucks everything, friend and foe alike. The Mobi was dead and his thrusters were stuttering. A couple of other sharks tumbled nearby, like Dallas caught in the circuit-numbing burst.

On the bright side, most of the Banu guns fell silent. A handful way aft were still barking in random directions, their targeting systems likely pointing at a distant star in pulse-addled confusion.

Gotta move, Dallas thought. *That state of disarray won't last forever.* The second wave of sharks would be here in moments, the ones that hung back out of reach of the Warlock.

Dallas watched the hull of the *Co'Ral* loom larger, a football stadium of sparks and stuttering lights. In an unbroken stream of bitching he pounded his fist against the EVA controls, when a huge ball of metal suddenly thundered just above his head like a mac truck roaring over a rabbit in the road.

Dallas recognized the tail; the *Red Revenge*. One engine still ablaze, her noseless corpse plowed into the side of the Merchantman. The vacuum of space sucked the fireball into twisting orange ribbons that fluttered and vanished.

What was left was a hole, about the size of a garage door, half-jammed with Cutlass wreckage. But half-jammed was half-open and Dallas got a short burst of jet, enough to push him closer to the ad hoc entry. He slammed into the *Co'Ral*, grabbing hold before he bounced back into space. Scrambling hand-over-hand, he pulled himself into the gaping wound.

He bit down against the scream that rose in his throat as the jagged knife-edge of a torn hull plate carved a deep furrow through the meat of his thigh. The pain was followed by the sudden nausea of suit decompression before the ring-bladder inflated and pressure-sealed around the top of his leg. An auto-infuser shoved painkillers into his bloodstream. The leg fell numb and a haze wrapped around his brain, but he was still functional.

Dallas snarled through gritted teeth and rolled through the rest of the hole, magboots getting an unsteady grip on the *Co'Ral's* deck floor.

A quick glance revealed that the demise of the *Red Revenge* bought him a lucky break. The explosive decompression caught the *Co'Ral* in the grip of EMP haze, so automatic bulkheads up and down the hall had failed to slam shut. Of the dozen crewmen he could see along the length of the dark corridor, none had the chance to get into space suits. They sprawled sightless, mouths agape, with no air in their lungs to scream.

Another man might have found that tragic. Dallas looked at it as ammo he didn't have to burn. Bummer news for the crew of the *Red*, but somebody had to take one for the team.

Dallas ambled as fast as a rubber leg would allow, heading down to cargo bay three. That's where the mercs would be holed up, some kind of elite guard according to the intel Vane had bought. Forty guys, full armor and weapons; whatever it was they were guarding had to be some kind of valuable.

An elevator door opened, revealing half a dozen Banu in EVA suits. Based on the surprise etched across each visor, they weren't expecting to to find a pirate blocking the door, especially a pirate with a shotgun. The Kastak barked – three rapid blasts – and the elevator door closed quietly, hiding the sight of bloodspattered walls.

Dallas resumed his run, eyes sweeping up to the ceiling as the chatter of small arms began to echo throughout the ship. His brothers were here.

He reached the wide steel doors of cargo bay three, surprised to find them still closed. Any bunch of hardcore mercs worth their salt oughtta be suited up and taking control of the floor.

Something was wrong. The gears in Dallas' mind spun. *Then again…maybe wrong was so very right.*

The loss of atmo was unexpected. His eyes narrowed, following the seam of the door from floor to ceiling. If the guys inside haven't come out, maybe they got caught without EVAs. The door might be closed to keep the air inside. An evil grin drew across Dallas' face. It would be a pity, a downright shame, if those doors cracked open.

The trample of boots were thudding along the overhead catwalks by the time Dallas had pried the coverplate off the lock. He'd been hot-wiring doors back in Leir since he was a kid but the pain in his leg was getting worse, the sluggishness crawling up into his arms.

He was fumbling with the ground wire when a sudden arc crackled and the doors parted. Dallas staggered backwards, his shotgun swinging up to join the dozen or so other weapons leveled at the growing divide.

The vault-like doors slid open, settling into the wall with a dull metallic bang. Dallas stood slack-jawed in front of the first row of silhouettes, the muzzle of the Karstak slowly sinking towards the floor. He looked at Bulldog, who returned a confused shrug.

Dallas stepped forward, extending a gloved hand to tap one of the stone figures on the forehead. Polished jade eyes stared back from beneath the ornate, spiked helmet. The warrior stood at rigid attention, a wickedly curved halberd in his grasp. Around him, another thirty-nine stone figures stood unblinking watch, rank and file around what looked like an ancient, gilded casket.

"Hey Cap'n," Dallas spoke softly into the CommLink. "You aren't gonna believe this…"

EDWARD ISN'T HERE

Roxy's Place
Brimstone

"I need to see him."

Roxy didn't flinch when I leaned in close to whisper in her ear. Her eyes, like those of the pudgy Quartermaster seated across the table, were fixed on the manifests spread between them. Her response was so hushed it might have been telepathy.

"Not a good time, Doc."

I was in a hurry and pushed closer to repeat myself with emphasis, my cheek brushing faintly against the jet-black cascade of hair.

That was pushing my luck; I knew it and everybody else knew it. Nobody crowded Roxy, shoved themselves into her space when she was conducting business. Had I done so with a hand instead of a cheek I'd probably be short a few fingers already. Nug and Thorvald detatched from opposite walls, two thick slabs of meat who took just a step before she froze them with a glance, a near-imperceptible shake of the head.

Now Roxy and I had a very real friendship, one that traced back long before she became Roxanne Devereaux. Long enough for me to know I'd just cashed in a little credit on that account.

"I'm sorry Rox," my apology was sincere. It wasn't that she really gave a shit, but in a city of predators and thieves, control was a matter of perception. If she intended to survive in this hellhole, there had to be no question who was boss under her roof.

Roxy took a pronounced pause, then adjusted a price on one of the manifests. She pushed it across the table with a firm "Final offer."

The Quartermaster, the business front for some doubtlessly scurvvy ship, tried to keep up his game face, but wasn't kidding anybody. Pawing stubby fingers down a forked scar on his cheek he nodded, then pressed his thumb to the tablet. The deal was done.

Only then did Roxy turn to face me, her demeanor softening just a bit despite the raised eyebrow that told me I'd hear about it later. But she glanced towards the stairs and said "Second floor, near the back; you'll hear it." Then she added, "I'd knock first."

I nodded, a bit dramatically, the public gesture of deference noted by everyone around the room. Turning away, I imagined the faint smile that tugged at her lips. Roxy did love being queen.

There was a whole lot of noise at the top of the staircase, the kind of sounds that have filled bordello hallways for years. Bedframes bouncing on floors, faked moans, the slap of wet skin.

Halfway down the hall I stepped over Benny, one of a hundred burnout tweakers that crawled the gutters of Brimstone looking for their next hit. I'd jump-started his heart at least once, though truth be told I don't know why. Based on the glaze over his bloodshot eyes, the little shit had doubtlessly committed whatever deplorable acts were needed to pay for his demons one more time. That mental image would leave scars.

I reached the end of the hall. The sounds behind door number six were, in fact, different; crunch of footsteps across broken glass, tearing fabric. A whimper, the kind no actress pulls off in the heat of feigned passion.

I thumped my fist on the door. "Edward, I need to talk to you."

The sounds behind the door ceased, then I heard the groan of floorboards draw closer. The door cracked open and a single eye glared at me through the gap. The pit-bull voice growled "Edward isn't here."

I held the eye's stare with my own. "Then get him. This is important."

The eye took me in for a long moment, a bloodshot, storm-grey orb that ticked up and down as if sizing me up; for a fight perhaps, maybe for dinner. Then the door slammed shut and the commotion renewed, barked words and the rustle of cloth.

The door burst open and Sasha scurried out, half-wrapped in a bedsheet and nothing else. She was thirty that I knew of, probably older, but the senesence inhibitors had stunted her development somewhere around twelve or thirteen. Another case of industrial science adapting to meet a market demand no matter how sordid, a seemingly odd necessity that was driven by Roxy's 'no kids' rule. You could pursue debauchery in infinite variety under her roof, but lay a hand on a kid, a real kid, and Roxy would have you put out an airlock.

Sasha rounded the door and scampered off down the hall, a glaring red handprint fanned across the curve of her bare ass. I turned back into the room where a buck-naked Edward stood at the dresser, cigarette clenched between his teeth as he fumbled with a near-empty bottle of scotch.

"This had better be fuckin' good." he growled, spitting the cig to the floor to throw back a slug of liquid amber.

I crossed the room towards the only chair, stepping over a crumpled white knee-high sock. Handcuffs dangled from the arm of the chair, much like the ones that hung from the headboard. I plucked what looked like a pleated belt of plaid fabric off the seat cushion, realized it was a skirt, and tossed it aside before settling in.

"How's your Ancient Philology?" I asked.

Edward turned. Despite the lingering scowl I knew it was Edward now, the color of his eyes had softened back to a more conventional blue. He pointed at the bed. "You interrupted THAT for some sort of language lesson?"

"Hey, you're the fucking priest."

Edward bristled at the word, flipping me the bird along with the glare he served up when he knew I was trying to get his goat.

'Priest' was a misnomer, something that got fucked-up in translation between the Xi'An and English. For us a priest was, well, a priest. Some holy guy who had god on speed-dial. Didn't matter what faith, if a group had a belief, you could be sure someone had carved an exclusive on correspondence with the Top Dog. When they weren't fondling altar boys or dipping into the till, humans priests were ostensibly keepers of traditions, interpreters of the signs, shit like that.

The Xi'An saw things a little different. Stories weren't passed down from one generation to the next through oral tellings, writings or holovids. The Xi'An kept history alive by downloading the memories of an old priest into the brain of a new one.

The transfer didn't over-write the recipient, just added a Search Engine full of data that became part of their combined consciousness. With each generation, the download got larger, the lives of each priest blending into the whole.

Ed, more formally Edward VII, had stuff from six prior Eds running around in his brain. The first two were Xi'An, followed by four humans. Thats a hell of a lot of knowledge, insight and firsthand experience sloshing together in one brainpan.

What they don't tell most folks is that when you mix memory pools, you can't exactly distill factual knowledge from the rest of life. So along with six Eds worth of study and learning, he inherited slices of obsession, addiction, of kinks and fetishes, angers and fears. The shit we all have but nobody admits.

Priests train for it, they are taught how to vent steam to maintain equillibrium and such. The Xi'An brains seem much better suited to sorting shit into its proper stacks.

They started the whole cultural exchange thing centuries ago, to promote better understanding across all the allied races. That notion came off the rails pretty early. The second Banu priest went apeshit on a scale that would make Hannibal Lecter queasy. Banu don't participate in the program any more.

Ed flopped down on the bed, grimacing as he fished one of Sasha's props – a tan teddy bear with a pink bow-tie – out from under his ass. He used it to scratch his balls, then tossed it aside and looked at me while lighting another smoke.

I'd seen Ed do far worse, but I still shook my head. "I gotta tell you Ed; collectively you are one sick motherfucker."

Ed blinked for a moment, then glanced at the smudged bear and gave a dour laugh. He tapped a finger against the side of his skull. "You got a problem with how things run in here, take it up with former management." Then he leaned forward, resting elbows on his knees. "So, what do you know, or think you know?"

I toggled on my MobiGlas and tried to pronounce the cypher as best I could. What came out sounded like a strained *"ermahgerd…"*

Ed winced, waving me to silence as if in pain. "Lemme see it."

I pulled out my wallet and flipped it onto the near end of the bed. The ID projector tossed an image of me into the air, along with my vital stats. Most if it was bullshit, but an ID was something you needed if you planned to travel outside of Leir space. I pushed a neural command and the Mobistream data fed out to the projector. A series of glyphs assembled in the air.

Ed's eyes narrowed and he took another long drag on the cig. "Where'd you find this?"

"Came out of somebody's head," I replied, the statement not entirely untrue.

Ed raised one eyebrow at me. "I don't suppose I could talk to this guy…"

"Yeah," I stammered, thinking about the severed noggin. "That's not gonna work."

Ed nodded, chewing on the smoke. "Figured as much." He paced around the cloud of symbols. "This all of it?"

"No," I answered, "just the tip of the iceberg. Most of it is machine language, engineering diagrams, bluerints. But I can't figure out what for." I pointed at the shimmering codex. "This was at the top."

Hm, Ed paced, oblivious to the bits of broken glass under his bare feet. His eyes shifted through shades of color. "Looks Futhark."

"If you mean FUBAR, I'm right there with ya."

Ed's gaze broke from the image, centering on me for a moment before he scowled and shook his head with an unspoken *"idiot…"* Then he took a breath and pointed at the top row of figures.

"Futhark. Old norse alphabet, tracks back centuries. I'll spare you all the Unification Theory bullshit but there are similarities between written languages, even theologies, that cross racial barriers between humans. Christ was cruficied on a wooden cross, Odin was hung on a tree. Completely different religious systems that shared odd similarities."

I nodded blankly.

"So zoom forward a few centuries and spread that net a hundred million light years. The old Xi'An kanaform script shares about fifty percent of its primary glyph structure with, guess what? Futhark runes. You got fourth century Vikings and sci-fi space lizards using the same damn alphabet. Sure, stylized as hell, but tied together. Writing leads to words, words lead to ideas. You go back far enough and you find very similar stories in cultures separated by galaxies."

"So what's it say?"

Ed rubbed the scruff on his chin. "It's sort of amalgam…"

"Best guess Ed."

He looked at me, clarity in his eyes now. Seven Eds worth of brain were cranking in high gear. He reached up, fingers tracing a loop around a central grouping of symbols.

"*Mòrì*, at least it's pretty close. That's a big event in Xi'An mythology." Then he widened the loop. "You add back these two symbols on the left and one on the right and you have the same basic thing in futhark runes, only the vikings called it *Ragnarok.* "

Ed scratched his head, voice somber. " Götterdämmerung, Armageddon, Shiva, hell Frodo versus Sauron; every race on every world has some sort of eschatology, some view of how it ends."

"How what ends?"

Ed gave me a cold stare. "Everything."

WE INTERRUPT THIS PROGRAM

Baachus : Astaroth City

INN COMLINK 27A-PR1
2945.08.04.1630 SOL
LIVE FEED: RIGGS/SAMANTHA 00324
[CLOSED CAPTION INCLUDED]

<TRANSCRIPT>

[STATIC] "-onditions in the streets of Baachus, the Banu homeworld, are understandably tense. With the G3 Summit on Refugee Relocation only days away, the timing of the *Co'Ral* Incident could not have been any worse."

[PROTESTORS CHANTING]

"The exodus of populations from all along the edge of Vanduul space, most notably systems like Elysium and Odin, continues to overwhelm immigration authorities across the G3.

Add to that the lack of UEE public policy with respect to unclaimed, developing or contested systems and 'The Displaced' have become one of the most serious civilian issues facing the current administration as it struggles to cope with the growing war effort."

"To make matters worse, the theft of the *Co'Ral*, which the Xi'An are calling a crime of 'immense cultural proportions,' threatens to throw gasoline on what is already a large fire. While delegates from each of the primary G3 partners are quick to point fingers around the table, public resentment has largely focused on the UEE, whose glaring foreign policy failures have been characterized as to blame for the influx of piracy in the region.

Given the disproportionate number of humans involved in this predation, and the permissive nation-state created by the tear-away Outsider republic, the crowds here in Baachus are looking to the Empire for answers. In the meantime, the UEE State Department has issued a travel advisory warning all non-essential UEE personnel to avoid the following regio—"

[LOUD EXPLOSION]

</TRANSCRIPT>

"Sam!!! Are you all right?"

Owen sounded like he was under water. He death-gripped the handle on the back of Sam's tac vest, hefting her to her feet.

Samantha looked him in the eyes and nodded, still trying to clear the cobwebs that wrapped her brain in fuzz. She blinked several times before she realized that the static across her vision was the AUG, trying to stream scrambled visor-overlay from the camera in her helmet. With a growl she smacked the heel of her palm against the side of her head and the AUG stream cleared.

Her brain cleared as well. Training kicked in and Sam dropped to one knee, yanking Owen down behind the solid bumper of the INN SatCom van. She had earned her stripes covering two different warfronts and knew all too well what happenes to people who stand up and gawk when the shit hits the fan.

"Kenny!" She barked loudly, "are we still on?" No answer. She reached back, thumping her fist on the van's back door.

"I'm alive!" Kenny's muffled shout echoed from inside the metal box. "Thanks for asking." Just a heartbeat passed before he added. "Main dish is fucked, I'm trying to get an LOS-Link off one of the towers. But we're recording local – so go!"

Sam didn't hesitate. By the sound of things, Kenny was fine. She was far more concerned about Owen, who despite his immediate heroics was looking a little woozy. Her alarm rose when she spotted a thin trail of blood working its way down from his left ear, crawling towards his shirtcollar.

Not a frag wound, she assessed, a little skill she had picked up from a medic on Centauri. Owen wasn't wearing a helmet when the blast hit; shockwave probably busted one of his eardrums.

She leaned in, watching closely as the spotlight on her camera swept across Owen's eyes. Right pupil tightened up, left one hung open. *Fixed and dialated.*

She thumped him on the chest with an open hand. "You're done. In the van, now."

Owen tried to push her back, then gazed at his own hand as he flexed his fingers several times. He looked up, wobbled unsteadily, dawning concern rising above his confusion. Still, he managed to force a stern, paternal look.

"Don't do anything stupid."

Sam fired back a quick grin. "Me? Never."

As Owen climbed into the van Sam turned and broke off at a dead run, keeping her head below the height of the vehicles parked up and down the street. She maintained the headlong pace for a good hundred meters, pulling up beneath the plaque on a memorial statue of one Gul' DuThar, the blah blah blah of some historic Banu... thing. Long ago. For now she was just thankful 'ol Gul merited an onyx pedestal that made for decent cover.

Cautiously, Sam peered out from behind that cover, the camera on her helmet sucking in the scene. Although she wasn't streaming live, she knew to narrate in a real-time style. That made for hi-drama replayability. It made for award-winning journalism.

"Some sort of bomb has just detonated in the crowd." She swept a wide establishing shot before zooming in to pick up details of the carnage. "Easily a dozen dead and wounded are littered around the plaza, suffering from injuries consistent with an anti-personnel weapon."

Her time on the Vanduul front had given her a first-hand lesson on the power of frag. Today's IEDs placed less emphasis on burns, instead betting the house on filling a crowd of soft targets with dense little pellets humming along at supersonic speeds.

She focused her lens on the side of a plumber's panel truck where a handful of neat round dents pocked the sidemetal. Good B-roll material.

The blare of sirens rolled up from the west; a stampede of police, fire and EMS personnel. Given the multi-national nature of the G3 Summit, the response would likely include military units as well. She looked up, noting three of the black, high-speed drones already circling the plaza.

Shifting her weight Sam rocked around the opposite side of the stone pedestal, giving her an unobstructed view up the rust-colored grass to the capitol steps where Secret Service personnel hustled half a dozen dignitaries away behind a moving wall of quick-deploy shield bots.

While the bomb wreaked havoc along the edge of the parking lot, it failed to reach across the hundred and thirty meters or so to the dias.

"Yep, the politicians walk while the working man takes it in the teeth." Sam didn't record that last statement; there are some truths that don't make for good holovision. Or good careers.

The first cop vehicles slid into the parking lot, low level blue-suiters who likely were half a block away pulling traffic detail. But the SWAT guys were right behind, their up-armored trucks built to survive a blast like the one that just took place. Black-armored stormtroopers bailed out of the van, compact carbines at the ready, forming a perimeter around the parking lot.

Sam rolled tape on the whole process, running color commentary on the growing crowd of cops, paramedics, firefighters and onlookers. Somebody spotted fuel leaking from three or four vehicles parked along the street, internal storage cells perforated by what was almost certainly a vest-full of ball bearings.

Fearing that some spark would start a conflagration, the fire guys rolled in a bright yellow MagLev with the word SUPPRESSANT stenciled along the side. A guy in white Level-C's clambored up the tail ladder and swung twin chrome nozzles that, with the yank of a lever, began to belch a thick expanding foam. The response was textbook, picture-perfect.

So why are the hairs crawling up the back of my neck?

Sam had learned to trust her instincts, to rely on they way her brain processed small details. That instrinct was twitching like mad.

She spun the AUG stream in reverse, backpedaling through the sequence of events. Foam sucked back into the nozzles. Medics backpedaled from the dying. Black-suiters flowing ass-first into the armored SWAT van. Cops reverse-fishtailed out of the parking lot. Slow sweep across people, pause on the dented truck panel.

Sam froze, the image hanging in front of her like a ghost.

The white plumber's truck was dimpled, not perforated like every other vehicle. SWAT armors their vans to absorb that kind of damage, but why would a plumber's van have an armored side? Her eyes went wide.

Adrenaline hit her system as Sam rolled from behind the cover of the monument and screamed, to everybody at once:

"RUUUUUUN!!!"

INN COMLINK 27A-PR1
2945.08.04.2230 SOL
LIVE FEED: DELMAR/KENNETH 887235
[CLOSED CAPTION INCLUDED]

"We interrupt this program to bring you breaking news from the scene of today's terrorist incident at the site of the G3 summit. Following a suicide-vest attack at 1632 EST, a second and much larger explosive device, confirmed now to have been hidden in what authorities have described as a white panel truck, detonated at 1644. The attack, apparently staged with an intimate knowledge of emergency responder protocols, has claimed 62 lives, largely police, fire and medical personnel.

Twenty-six-year-old Samantha Riggs, a beloved member of the INN family and two-time Zelnik Award Winner, was one of those killed in the attack."

THE BANU SEND THEIR REGARDS

Deep Space - Garron System

A prudent man makes it his business to notice the little things; especially things like tiny bits of brain and polymer splattered above a doorway. In the cold dark of space, details like that can be important.

Given the haste with which the space-suited figure EVA'd towards the access portal of Comm Array Two-Seven-Niner, the guy centered in my riflescope was anything but prudent. No surprise really, outlaws don't exactly screen for intelligence.

I shifted, my crosshair sliding left to settle on the Cutlass that was parked like a remora beneath a wide expanse of Two-Seven-Niner's solar panel. The velvet black hull told me she was wrapped in that rubbery, sensor-absorbant coating; the kind of shit that helps you sneak up on people. The Cutlass sat cold, engines at low idle, cockpit lights out.

These were not your run-of-the-mill vandals ripping circuit breakers out of a Comm Array for laughs. And they weren't common low-lifes cannibalizing a unwatched station for sellable parts. This was a back-up team, checking up on a guy who'd gone silent.

I allowed myself a faint grin. *He's gotta be inside, right guys? I mean, that's his Avenger parked beneath the other panel.*

I knew exactly where the other guy was. Well, the parts of him that weren't spattered above the doorframe. He and his friends were the reason I was out here.

Someone had been methodically shutting down relays in this sector for months now, creating blackouts in coverage that allowed smugglers – and far worse – to slip through the grid without observation. Normally that is just part of the cat and mouse chase that goes on out here.

That all changed when some crew of hardcores decided to hit a Banu hauler fat with a big-deal cargo. From all reports it was an ugly bit of work; no polite demands, no settle-this-shit-like-gentlemen. The hauler vanished, cargo vanished, crew presumed dead. And that pissed off some very rich, very important people.

People that hire people like me.

Given the stealthcoat on her hull, I had twenty bucks that said that somewhere in the guts of the Cutlass was a stolen MILCOM adapted to pirate frequencies. But a comms network pointed in two directions and tapping into a phone system can lead you to the caller. My employer wanted that box intact.

The objective of my little exercise wasn't to make a big, visible statement; it was to enable one.

I glanced back towards Hasty, pleased to see the glow of his headlamp disappearing into the Array's tunnel entrance. I had no intention of letting him actually reach the breakers; if I did I'd have to un-ass my hide and go reboot the damn thing myself.

That meant I had about about twelve seconds. I had clocked myself making the breaker run; thrusting along the curved passage in zero-G, rounding into the open inner core and diving down to the power panel. At door-plus-twelve seconds an intruder is just about as far from his ship as he can be without actually reaching the panel.

I'm a prudent man; I notice things.

I'd spent the last eight days floating out here in a custom-built hide that was to all outside appearance just another rock in space. Who would think to look for a signature-dampening capsule anchored to a baby asteroid? Chuck me out of the ass-end of a passing hauler and this rig of mine will latch onto a suitable piece of rock and bring the whole bundle to a drift that matches the target area. Once done, I'm just another piece of the environment.

My gaze flicked to the digits in the lower left of the scope. Habit I guess, the hard-edged discipline of check and re-check. I knew before looking that the range was just a touch over fourteen kilometers.

That sounds like a long-ass way, but truth be told, it is just a game of numbers.

Sniping has always been about the math. Back in the day, when warriors dressed like shrubs and crawled through planetside jungles, rifle shots were governed by a myriad of factors. Gravity, multiple winds, humidity, ballistic coefficient, even Coriolis Effect could play a role in a long shot. For centuries, 'long range' was a term defined in yards; well into the twentieth century a thousand yard shot was quite a feat.

But as tech advanced, engagements reached out to a mile or more. By the time one of those bullets hit its target, it had carved a serpentine path through three dimensions like a drunken snake. The math was insane.

None of that stuff mattered in space, where neither gravity nor air could play havoc with a bullet's trajectory.

The bullets themselves held little resemblance to the sleek, tapered projectiles of old. Today a short osmium rod packed the highest amount of mass into a cylindrical form factor.

Beyond its incredible density, fine osmium particles – the kind you get when a bullet disintegrates on impact – will act like Greek Fire in the presence of oxygen. In the right conditions you get a natural armor-piercing incendiary.

They ain't cheap but, damn… they are spectacular.

Ten of those rods, each a whopping 1200 grains in weight under normal 1G, lay nestled in Christine's magazine. She was my baby, a custom LR-620 originally built by Klaus & Werner. The polished rails were overclocked fourteen percent over MIL-SPEC, thanks in large part to a high-density capacitor pack that ran the length of her underbarrel.

The scope was an upgrade as well, swapping out the Marine Corps "lowest bidder" glass for a top-of-the-line Behring PSG-1. That's a lot of shop talk to say that my sweet little Christine was the Princess of Fucking Darkness if you happened to be downrange.

In atmo, where air and grav start to drag at a bullet the moment it leaves the muzzle, Christine could punch a burning hole through forty mils of plate armor from three thousand meters out. But here in the black, with nothing but vacuum between me and my target, a bullet can go a whole lot farther.

That's where the math comes back in. Riflescopes back on Earth worked in MOA, minutes of angle. At a thousand yards, a one-MOA error could put your bullet about a quarter-meter off target, not so good when your average human is barely half a meter wide at the shoulders.

At a range of fourteen klicks, that same one-MOA error widens out to over one and a half football fields; five times the length of the Cutlass. Hitting something at that distance was a game of infinitely tiny fractions, or just sheer luck. Off by a hair at the muzzle is off by a mile at the target.

Of course, I didn't believe in luck. The mantra of sniper school was "if you ain't cheating, you ain't trying."

My thumb rode across a small switch that spun up the gyro stabilizers in Christine's stock. Yeah, the motors would give off a slight magnetic signature, maybe enough to escape the cloaking metal coffin that surrounded me. But nobody would be around long enough to notice.

I pushed the scope, zooming in on the trapezoid of ballistic glass that defined the Cutlass' forward canopy. I was thankful for the side-shot; the steep rake of her upper pane could glance an incoming round, even one coming in as hot as this.

At a neural command my armor quietly went rigid, fusing rifle, shooter and asteroid into one solid form as my finger drew back on Christine's trigger. She responded with a soft, throaty *thunk*.

The big railguns, naval ship weapons, can hurl a car-sized round scorching downrange at Mach 15. Christine couldn't match that, but she could throw a thumb-sized rod of metal at Mach 9. At that speed it took just over five seconds for the slug to hit the glass.

The canopy exploded inward, spalling transparent shards through the cockpit. You don't have to see the pilot, much less hit him directly, when you can fill his compartment with a cloud of hypervelocity razor blades.

The Cutlass vented atmo in a gush of dying breath, pushing her nose in a dead-stick drift to starboard. A small chuff of satisfaction escaped my lips as I swung the crosshair back to the Comm Array's front door. It wasn't likely the pilot got off a warning, but Hasty would know real quick that his radio went dead. He'd damn sure feel the crunch when the nose of the Cutlass scraped against the side of the station.

A tiny grin tugged at my lip; another twenty bucks says Hasty beats his inbound time getting back out.

The corridor began to glow as a headlamp swung madly from her depths. My crosshair was centered on the opening when Christine barked again, a second bolt hurtling across the void.

Five. Four. Three…

In times of uncertainty, a prudent man would have paused; taken a moment to peer out from behind cover and size things up. Hasty didn't stop until he saw his ship rolling belly-up beneath him.

He was standing like that when the bullet hit him square in the chest and another layer of vaporized chunks sprayed across the doorway.

Looking through the scope I watched the crimson mist dissipate into the void, flecks of red ice. Before toggling the beacon that would call in the clean-up crew I said the words, just as I was instructed.

"The Banu send their regards."

THINGS WE LEAVE BEHIND

The Nekropolis, Brimstone

With a groan Dutch screwed both fists into his temples, as if with enough force he could squeeze the pain from his skull. Flecks of vomit stuck to his teeth, the stench of rotten eggs in the air made worse by the funk of his own belly acid. Wheezing hard he doubled over, dropped to one knee, retching until slimy threads drooled from his mouth and nose.

Gotta get home.

Far easier said than done, Dutch realized, sitting alone in the dark. There was no moonlight, only the glow of distant building lights to carve the street into smears of gloom and utter black. Dragging a stained sleeve across his face, Dutch tried to focus on the nearest silhouettes. A wilted antenna, a burned-out PTV, the entrance to a mine shaft.

The pavement was rough beneath his palms and crunched as he shifted his weight. Dutch closed his fist and the layer of ash crumbled in his grasp, black dust sifting between his fingers.

Fire.

The word appeared in his mind as both question and answer. The whole street looked like it had been blasted to hell and worked with a flamethrower. Even the ground was hot.

But I don't remember a fire.

As sick as he felt, Dutch was pretty sure he had not been burned, at least nowhere he could see. Nothing of this nightmare made any sense. He needed answers, to talk to somebody. Anybody.

Where's Lenny… or Falco? And where the hell is Camber?

With a groan Dutch pushed himself upright and the world swayed as his reward. His work-worn Timberlands felt like size-12 cinderblocks as he stumbled lead-footed into a compressor, its sheetmetal surface every bit as crusted as the asphalt. Trails of black dust kicked up as his forearms slid across the top of the machine.

"C'mon Marine!" He hissed the words through clenched teeth. "Pull your shit together." The sound scraped like sandpaper across his raw vocal chords before quickly succumbing to hoarseness. It had been twenty years since he left the Corps, but once a Marine, always a Marine.

So make a fucking plan; figure out where you are.

He wasn't in the yard, that much was certain. Even torched and twisted like some fucked-up impressionist painting, the factory where he worked every day would still be familiar. He'd recognize the layout of the yard, steel frames stacked in rows along the fenceline. The forklift…

Dutch's right hand slid down to his hip, pawing for the Schrade clipped to his belt. The heavy five-inch knife wasn't much in terms of a weapon but the feel of it in his hand was a comfort. Eyes peering into the darkness, he thumbed the blade open with a soft click. *Oorah.*

Bolstered ever so slightly, Dutch choked down a wad of spit and headed for the street corner, following a stretch of unbroken pavement. The city grid display was blackened like everything else, the once-smooth diode screen now warped and cracked. A dense smoke hugged the ground, thick and pungent, cutting his vision to no more than a hundred paces.

From what little Dutch could see, the city center of L1B had been reduced to ruin. Burned, busted, melted, whatever. He struggled to remember what happened when a dark thought crossed his mind. Could it be, was it possible that… that nobody else survived?

Dutch pushed himself into a foreward stride, wobbling one crunchy step after another like a drunk on Saturday night. Only the frequent collisions kept him upright as he pinballed off a wall, a trash bin, against a pile of rubble. In his focus to walk he passed the motionless figure, staggering a couple steps beyond before the shape of the man registered.

"Oh fuck, am I glad to see you—" Dutch croaked, then the words stalled on his lips.

The figure stood motionless, a craquelure silhouette of dark pumice with arms raised in front of its face. The detail was unearthly; every button and fold of fabric rendered in porous black stone. Steam seeped from cracks in its chest and arms.

Dutch vaguely remembered some ancient myth about a creature whose gaze could turn a man to stone, but this was no fairy tale. Very real terror was etched into the statue's petrified expression, gloss black eyes forever wide with fear.

Everything inside Dutch wanted to explode; his body tried to scream, puke and shit his drawers all at once, but the synapses all tangled up. What he did instead was run; a blind, arm-flailing dash.

He wasn't sure how far he ran, how many twists and turns he had taken, how many charred bodies he passed along the way. Figures of men, women, even a dog. He knew his lungs burned, that his right hand ached from the white-knuckle grip on the Schrade.

But then, through the fog, he spotted something familiar. Tucker's welding shop was still standing. T's old pickup, or what was left of it, was still parked in the loading bay. Dutch looked left, right, matching details to memory.

Yeah, fuck yeah. I know where I am!

His own factory was just two blocks away, down that alley. Dutch plodded faster, the first shred of hope catching hold in his chest.

He'd covered half the distance when movement caught his eye, the unexpected drift of shadows overhead. Dutch skidded to a stop and looked up as two figures plodded along the raised walkway. One was huge, thick-featured; towering over the other, every few steps giving the smaller man a gentle nudge to move him on his way. They paused at a landing and Dutch shouted, waved his arms, but neither figure seemed to notice.

For a moment Dutch looked frantically for a rock, a can, something to throw. He grabbed a beer bottle in the gutter but it was fused to the ground and refused to budge. The two men were close enough that Dutch could almost make out their voices.

Why the hell can't they hear me?

The answer was not what Dutch expected. Not what any sane mind would have expected. The big guy took the lead and started down the metal stairs. With each step, they became increasingly transparent. Before they reached the next landing, both men disappeared completely.

Dutch felt his blood turn to ice; the sensation drained from his limbs. This was not some trick of the smoke, he didn't blink or miss something. The stairs were just as clear then as they are now. It was the men that vanished, the sound of their footsteps evanescing into the wind's soft moan.

Dutch didn't believe in ghosts or gorgons but the shit he'd seen today whispered of both. Motionless, breathless, he stared at the walkway.

They just... faded away.

Dutch never took his eyes off the catwalk, finally edging forward until he saw the gold wings of Revel & York on the corrugated metal wall. He slipped through the side door, crossing the factory floor strewn with tools and out into the yard.

A distant glimmer sparked. That's where he'd last seen the guys. They were palletizing a shipment of hangar frames. Falco was bitching about something. The weight; it was the weight of the beam.

Dutch rounded the back of the forklift and froze in his tracks. Lenny was there all right, standing alongside Falco and Camber. They were braced up against a three-meter section of T-beam.

No, Dutch realized sourly. *They were... part of it. Shoulders passing through steel or... metal passing through flesh... Maybe both.*

Dutch looked up, a jumble of sights and sounds coalescing in his mind. Something in the sky, something awful. His brow furrowed as he tried to put words to the sight.

A ball of... writhing voltage.

His nerves remembered how the night air had burned with a furnace-like heat. And that noise, that sucking howl like a rabid tornado. Dutch remembered how it tore at him, how it tried to peel him out of the forklift… peel him out of his own flesh. How he screamed as he held on for all he was worth, until the relentless force tore him away and swept him into the maelstrom.

Tears streaking his face, Dutch stared into the distance. Even darker images lingered on the edge of his mind, the fading remnants of nightmare. Tall demonic figures with leathery hides, eyes that burned like embers in the gloom. Monsters of teeth and tusks and claws that guarded the door to hell with wicked blades.

Dutch pushed the nightmare from his mind and gazed mournfully at the forklift… at the charred figure inside clutching the wheel in a deathgrip. He understood now, knew the ash-black remnants of Timberland boots were size twelve, that a Marine Corps tattoo once sprawled down the left arm, and that the knife fused into the charred belt was a Schrade.

And with that he knew… he was never getting home.

PREACHER, PROPHET, SOLDIER, SPY

Mine 3, The Nekropolis, Brimstone

Ed held out a tumbler of translucent liquid. "Mucus?"

Given the unblinking stares from the Xi'An standing around the shrine I took the glass, snarling at Ed through a forced smile. "Funny."

I cautiously tipped the glass a few degrees, watching the viscous fluid resist the change in orientation, then leaned into his shoulder and asked "What is this stuff really?"

Ed gave me a sideways glance, one eyebrow cocked up for a moment before he nodded at the tumbler. "Mucus. Really. Polymer gel secreted by the Jīnshǔ kuài, a rare Xi'An gastropod." In response to what was doubtlessly a dead-blank look on my face, Ed clarified. "Snail slime. It's a delicacy. Drink up."

The line of green tortoise-faces raised their glasses, clearly waiting on my lead. Ed reached over and tinked his glass against mine. His grin was malevolent.

"There will never be an eighth Ed," I hissed, and threw back the glass.

The group followed suit with a rumble of throaty gullet-sounds I took for approval. I didn't utter a word, terrified that if my teeth unclenched the contents of my entire digestive tract would spray across the jade heads evenly spaced around the shrine. Odds are that would be some kind of insult.

Despite his obvious amusement at my expense, Ed got down to business, speaking to the group in some ancient Xi'An tongue, 'formal Zhou' he called it. The nasal, wet-sounding speech was supposedly the language of the enlightened, the highborn; not the trashy *Guóyǔ* spat out by the unwashed masses. To my ear it sounded like a frog hocking up a lunger.

I caught a few words here and there, phrases laced with that curt, head-forward nod they do, followed by a hand gesture in my direction and the word *'Jiàoshòu.'* More nods; I tried to return the gesture as best I could. Then I remembered the translator and tapped the device stuck in my right ear.

"– the course of a forensic examination, the Doctor discovered something curious, which he brought to my attention."

Ed had convinced me to stick as close to the truth as possible, at least until we had some idea what all this shit meant. We wouldn't lead with all of the details, but we'd be straight about the ones we did share.

With both hands Ed presented them with an envelope that contained a print of the futhark, which they accepted with equal formality. Apparently the act of reducing something to print gave it additional *gravitas* in Xi'An culture, made it a tad bit more valuable than just a block of digits in a memory brick. I watched carefully as they unwound the ribbon closure and pulled the holoprint into view.

Now I don't speak turtle and I sure as hell don't know my way around a *Shū lā*, but one thing I'm damn good at is poker. I saw spines stiffen up under layers of silk and brocade *hanfu*, watched eyelids draw back and nostrils flare.

One of the Xi'An, a lower-ranking member of the group standing to my immediate right, even sucked in a tiny croak. It was obvious that the holoprint hit the reptiles like a bad river card smacks a guy who just went all in.

From the center of the group Dàshǐ Kuang glared and made a dismissive gesture. His entourage bowed, backed away and scuttled off. In a moment only the three of us stood in the company of the Xi'An's revered dead.

A Dàshǐ was a cultural and religious ambassador of sorts, at least thats how it was pitched. But Ed had explained beforehand that Kuang was part of an order that, in Xi'An society, crossed various lines of authority; preacher, prophet, soldier, spy. It goes to reason that if you trust a guy to deliver the word of the gods, he was good to go with state secrets as well.

I was willing to bet that Kuang had some knowledge of the whole futhark thing, likely more than he wanted to tell. But I watched him lean forward, murmuring softly as he lit a tapered joss, and it struck me that he wanted to know more. There was about to be some horse-trading and unless I missed my guess, Kuang was deciding how much he was willing to ante up.

"*Mòrì,*" he said softly, still facing the shrine. A curl of smoke rose from the freshly lit incense.

Ed nodded, his voice somber. He paused for a moment, then said for my benefit: "Doomsday."

Kuang turned, his face as inscrutable as those of his carved-jade ancestors. "The Shèngjīng of Chong Whey…"

Watching my expression he paused, sighed, and re-set. "The scriptures of a revered prophet, speaks of the end times, the apocalypse, an event harbingered by the opening of the *Ménhù.*"

The translator hiccuped on the last word, a reference too obscure for its database. I looked at Ed.

"A portal," he said with a 'more or less' waggle of his hand. "Metaphorically a door, *Mén,* but back in the day *Ménhù Dìyù* was one of those terms that appeared in a number of religious writings. In English it would be something like the 'Gates of Hell'. "

Something like– I damn near swallowed my tongue. "That's not one of those terms that has a bunch of other meanings, is it?"

Ed shook his head slowly, expression dour.

If that left hook hadn't been enough, Kuang followed it up with a roundhouse right. "We believe the *Ménhù* is here."

For a moment the sense of surreal threatened to overwhelm me. Part of me wanted to laugh at the joke but nobody else was smiling. Then again, I was in a mineshaft below the Nek , talking with seven Eds in one brain and a six-foot turtle dressed in Kung-Fu movie robes. Why should the Gates of Hell seem at all implausible?

"Let me get this straight." I tried to regroup but couldn't manage the words, much less the concept. "You think a gateway… to Hell… is going to open up… right here?"

Kuang gave me a long, hard look, then turned to Ed. Something passed between them, unspoken but tangible. Kuang turned back to the shrine; it was Ed who spoke.

"Look, prophecy, religion, scripture, these things are a lot more literal in Xi'An culture than they are with mankind."

"What aren't you telling me Ed?"

He chuffed. "To get that answer you gotta tell me, are you in or are you out?"

"In or out of what Ed?"

He looked me in the eye, his demeanor turning to stone. "Everything Doc; down the rabbit hole, take the red pill, talk to the man behind the curtain. But..." he paused, "when I say there is no going back, I mean there isn't even a waver. You try to get off this train once it pulls out of the station, you even talk about the train to anyone, and things will go bad. Brutally bad. And there will be nothing I can do to stop it. Do you follow me?"

I tried to swallow but my throat tightened up. I'd seen a lot of Eds, watched that whole Jeykll-and-Hyde shift from academic robot to fetish sociopath, but I'd never seen anything like this. Ed didn't move, didn't raise his voice, but the vibe that emanated from him scared the shit out of me. I wanted to run and not look back; couldn't begin to imagine how I'd deal with Lazlo, who was already getting pissed with my delays.

My eyes swept the mined-out cavern, transformed by the Xi'An into something of a church. Ornate statues. Old books in glass cases. Candles by the hundreds. A whole lot of work went into this for a reason beyond my grasp. I had to know.

"I'm in." The words fell from my lips like somebody else had spoken them.

Kuang turned as if surprised by the suddenness of my decision. Ed nodded at him then looked back at me. "So here's the deal. Kuang wants you to go get the code, the rest of the data you got out of that guy's head. Bring it here and you become part of the Big Picture."

I nodded, reticent to appear uncertain. Kuang just stared back at me with those dark, still eyes. It was the kind of moment that called for some brilliant disclosure of cleverness and planning on my part and I had nothing. Instead I reached down and twisted the heel of my left boot, rocking it open to reveal a small compartment. The tiny data shard fell into my palm.

I tossed it to Ed. "It's all there."

Ed openly gaped. "That's it? The key to the End Times and you hid it in your boot?"

I shrugged.

Muttering under his breath, Ed held the shard up to the light as if it were a gem, then handed it to Kuang. With even less ceremony it disappeared into the folds of the Dàshǐ's silk robe.

Deal done, it seemed; *no signing a contract in blood required.*

Without a word Kuang walked past me, toward the mining elevator that had brought us down the fifty or sixty meters below the charred surface of the Nek.

A forceful glare from Ed told me that a polite invitation wasn't forthcoming so I took off after Kuang and followed him to the open-cage lift. But instead of rising back to the surface, the platform dropped into darkness.

I watched the shaft's old depth markers rise past us, tritium numbers that glowed in the dark. One hundred meters, two hundred, three... As we descended, the frozen cold of the planet's core overcame the inexplicable heat of the Nek. My breath began to fog.

I didn't look at Ed, instead asking the question aloud. "So do you realy buy into all this Gates of Hell stuff?"
Ed seemed to ponder the question for a moment. "Do I believe in it? Yeah, I guess I do. At least I'm not ready to dismiss things that people described long ago looking through a lens of limited science and understanding. Go back far enough and a light bulb would have been described as magic. A big part of what we priests do involves taking things on faith."

Without warning, the darkness of the mineshaft peeled away as the elevator descended through the roof of a massive underground cavern. The walls of the old mine hub stood several hundred meters apart, maglev rails extending off into a dozen side-tunnels.

Most of the chamber was damp and gloomy save where lights blazed in a circle around lab-coated Xi'An who moved among dozens of consoles wired together on the ground below. In the center of the chamber stood a claptrap array of metal arms that held emitters in a spherical pattern.

My heart stopped, images of the Brimstone holocaust twisting my guts like someone just ripped the bandaid off my memory. In the center of the emitters hung a ball of crackling energy; incandescent tendrils flickered outward in all directions.

"Then again," Ed added, "we're not stupid either."

GOOD FENCES MAKE GOOD NEIGHBORS

The Claddagh Pub, Brimstone

"Is not possible."

Yakov wasn't in the habit of saying *nyet* to Vane; an act which, in the wrong circumstance, could end with a sharp bit of steel shoved through your voicebox. Everyone in Brimstone knew the story that ended with a head on a post wearing a scrawled sign that read 'I angered Charles Vane.'

Vane barely seemed to notice the rebuff, his one good eye fixed on the shotglass in his hand. Dark mahogany swirled, catching what few lights burned in the dark bar before the pirate threw it back and slapped the empty glass on the table. He fixed his gaze on the burly Yakov and said "Find a way."

Yakov stroked his beard, an unkempt bush that added to the whole Russian Bear mystique. The problem was a minefield, a shitstorm waiting to happen. Then again, this was Vane.

Though he would never say it aloud, Yakov was one of the few men in Brimstone that knew Vane's real name. *Nom de Guerres*, pirate names, were common, especially among those who aspired to greatness or a long career. Advertising your real identity gave cops and enemies alike numerous free angles of attack.

Assumed names ran from the clever to the cryptic, from quirky handles to names drawn from antiquity. These days there must be thirty or forty Blackbeards, Calico Jacks, Anne Bonnys or Ching Shihs running around space, half of them trying to elbow their way into the limelight with the other half happy to get lost in the crowd.

But there was only one Charles Vane. After you butcher the first five or six imitations, people start choosing safer pseudonyms. Vane wanted there to be no confusion on who he was, or what he would do if challenged, and fuck any cop, Marine or merc who thought to put his resolve to the test. He'd been in pitched battles, suffered horrific injuries, but at the end of the day, Vane endured.

But this... Yakov wrestled with the idea; this was likely to be the death of everyone involved. "Cargo is too hot, too identifiable. Is not possible to sell it back to Banu, and no way you deal with fucking *Tortugas*." Yakov spat the last word. Three years rotting in a Xi'An prison can make a guy bitter.

Yakov watched Vane lean back in his chair, tapping a finger slowly on the tabletop. Even in his calm moments he exuded the air of a caged panther. The Russian had a keen eye for fighters, a lifetime obsession that had won him, and cost him, several small fortunes with bookies across the 'verse.

The pirate was a dichotomy; Vane stood under two meters tall, just on the high side of eighty kilos. Not massive, not a remarkable reach, but every ounce of living flesh was as iron-hard as Vane's refusal to die. There was something about Vane's eye, the human one anyway, that suggested he saw you not as a man, but as a collection of vital organs laced together by major arteries.

"Humor me." Vane's tone was soft, he even smiled, but somewhere between the lines was an air of menace.

Yakov scratched his head, putting aside a million things that could go wrong to focus on figuring out one way it might go right. His brows furrowed, then flared open.

"Maybe is one way. Slim maybe."

Vane's eye locked on Yakov with a laser-like focus that wordlessly said "Go on."

"I know a guy," then he grimaced, hand waving side to side. "Eeeehhh, no, not so much, I know OF a guy. Rich guy. Call him… Smith; is good name, no? So, some guys collect cars, boats; Smith collects history. Has sort of private museum, the kind you keep locked in basement.

Vane nodded thoughtfully. He knew the type; spend millions on rare art just to know they own it. What they can't buy, they pay somebody to steal. "So how do we get to this Smith?"

Yakov grunted, then pursed his lip. "Not easy, is private guy. Wary. I don't think so much he will talk to riff-raff pirate. Introduction will likely require a… demonstration."

Vane sat quietly for a moment as Megan, the bartender's daughter, stepped up and slid a fresh shot across the thick wooden table, collecting the seven or eight fallen soldiers that lay strewn across the oak battlefield. The pirate watched her walk away, lifted the glass, considered it for a moment, then drank it down, eye closing as he swallowed. When the orb re-opened, it revealed the panther within. Vane set the glass on the table and said with a fanged smile "Then we have to make a compelling statement."

Despite the insanity of it all, a smile crept across Yakov's face as he tapped into his Mobi Glas. This was his game. In simple terms yeah, he was a fence, a mover of stolen goods, a *purveyor of unclaimed cargo* in polite society.

But any idiot could do that, haggle low and sell high, eeking out an existence on the margin. A good fence – no, a *great* fence – was so much more. A great fence had a network, sometimes contracting sales in advance of acquisition. He would take orders from customers seeking every sort of commodity, from stolen goods to industrial secrets; commodities that drew breath… or ones from whom that capacity should be taken away. Yakov was a finder, a fixer, a contractor who made it his business to know the business of others; their needs, their wants… and their vulnerabilities.

Yakov paused, a news article Mobi-floating in his vision. "Hm, our friend has *vrag*, ah, political enemy." The Russian snorted "Pah! Zillionaire idiots poking each other in sandbox. Only this, what is name... ah, Zul-Ren. He is making very public this fight. Social media, televid. For men like Smith, public is cancer."

"Carving out a tumor sounds like a pretty good door-opener."

"Da," Yakov replied, "Must be clean, how you say... *squeaky*." The Russian suddenly took a dour turn. "But solution still leaves problem. Even if we can move goods to Smith invisibly, authorities will never stop looking. Somewhere, someday that search leads to you. One day you get knock on door and is not girly-cookies they are selling."

Vane smiled quietly as he leaned forward, resting muscled forearms on the table. "As amusing as that sounds, I see your point. We gotta make the feds, the mercs, all believe that —"

The sound of breaking glass stopped Vane in mid-sentence. Both men turned to look across the dark bar where a table lay on its side. Some scrawny dock rat, a Krokodil junkie by the looks of him, was backed into the corner, raised arms lined with track marks.

"Jake, you gotta believe me, I'd never sell you out."

Jake, at least the guy to whom the cornered wretch was speaking, was flanked by two figures on either side.

Roughnecks, Vane surmised, all armed but short of that armed-to-the-teeth look of professional killers. Jake was solid, bigger than Vane, and carried the scars of somebody who'd been dragged around the block a few times. Still, Jake was a dwarf compared to the guy on the far right, a damn mountain of muscle.

But it was the girl who moved first, stepping forward with a straight right that whiplashed the addict's skull off the wall. The wet crunch of bone made tough guys around the bar wince.

Eyes glazed, the junkie's face lolled with a nose crushed to one side, blood streaming across his teeth. The girl stepped back, flexing her fist, anxious to throw another.

Vane looked at Yakov and grinned. "I like her style."

Jake spoke to the mountain, who lifted the bloody, mewling addict by the throat. As a group they turned and made for the exit, hauling their prize like a bag of groceries. Jake paused and spoke to the Fitz the barkeep. A wad of folded bills passing in the handshake. Then Jake took a last look around the room and left.

Vane looked at Yakov, still amused. "What was that?"

The Russian grinned. "Jake Brogan, captain of *Goliath*, big ship with arm..."

"Reclaimer."

Yakov nodded, pointing a finger at Vane. "Da. They run salvage; sometimes run... other things." Yakov narrowed his eyes at Vane. "Ah, the fiery one; she is Jesse. You two see eye-to-eye I think."

Then the Russian's face turned sour, "The maggot is Welker, little piece of *der'mo*. He owes Jake money, well, owes lots of people money. Over last couple days he brags that he is smart guy, sends Jake and crew to their death, clears his chit. Only now it appears…"

"Jake didn't die."

The Russian chuckled. "Da. Jake is like you that way, he has *umeniye*, a knack, for survival. Like you too, he has bad temper. Welker's survival chances now, I think, not so good."

"This Jake, is he reliable?"

Yakov snorted. "What, you are in scrap business now?" Then he waved the joke away. "Da, they are solid crew, very loyal. Maaaybe die for each other, certainly kill for each other. But very under the radar, how you say, look very legit. As for reliable, da. If Jake tells you will be done, is done."

"Interesting," said Vane as he motioned Fitz for another round. "So back to this Smith of yours and his enemies…"

NO-KNOCK WARRANT

Shipyard Block G37, Brimstone

"Tiger Team you are go in three, two, one."

From a rooftop a block out a suppressed rifle chuffed on the 'wuh' of 'one.' Dyson didn't hear the shot, but the back of Greyshirt's head burst like a melon and he dropped, a puppet with cut strings. At go-plus-two Dyson was already up the short flight of stairs, exo-skeleton driving long strides, when the next precision shot dropped Tattoo in the parking lot on Side 4.

"Two in the box, two in the box." Dyson barked on the secure comm.

An icon for each member of Tiger Team defined the four corners of Dyson's HUD, all bright green. Zach and Connor would be hard-charging the garage door on Side 4 while Dyson and Sego took the front with Lance on overwatch with the rifle.

Who says we're not ready for this shit, Dyson sneered.

Pivoting, Dyson pressed himself against the wall on the hinge-side of the door while Sego swung the muzzle of the breacher's gun over the doorlock. A modified 40mm grenade launcher, the gun fired a flatbody projectile, something that could drive a deadbolt through an armored door. Sego pulled the trigger.

Despite the cannon-bang of the gun, the door exploded outward instead of in, a burst of shards and buckshot scorching between the two bounty hunters. Dyson dropped flat, swinging the stubby carbine up as he kicked. His boot connected and the splintered door swung inward, revealing a black-jacketed shooter some three meters inside.

A sharp whine scorched over Dyson and blackjacket toppled backwards, the auto-shotgun falling to the floor.

Dyson snapped a quick glance over his shoulder, throwing a rapid thumbs-up to the sniper. *Out of sight, but never out of range.*

Sego was bleeding but it wasn't bad, a pellet or two had carved furrows across the outside of his left bicep. Dyson wasn't taking any chances and pulled a grenade from his vest. He yanked the pin and lobbed it into the room with a loud 'stun out'. The sphere skipped off the wall before the gyromotor kicked in, accelerating it across the floor towards the greatest concentration of heat signatures. Dyson turned his head as the dark room went white.

He was through the door before the echo of the blast subsided, Sego on his heels. Despite the smoke and chemical haze from the grenade, thermal images wobbled on Dyson's visor. The room was a workshop, most of the walls were lined with benches and tool chests. Half the things lying about looked dangerous; acetylene torch, arc-welder, nail gun, plasma saw.

Well, Dyson thought with a malevolent mirth, *they're only dangerous if somebody is alive to use 'em.*

Dyson's AR barked in short, controlled bursts, the first tearing holes through a glass-beading booth. The figure hiding behind it was knocked from a crouch to an awkward sprawl. The spray of hot blood showed white in infrared.

Twenty-three second in, seven in the box counting kills streaming up from the floor below, no team casualties. As far a high-risk no-knocks go, things were running right on plan.

Fuck you Old Man, who'se the Big Dog now?

Jäger was a legend, no question. One of the best bounty hunters to ever stuff a perp in a freezer. That's how you end up running a training center like Magnum Force. But Jäger was old and grey now, in Dyson's mind a dinosaur from an age gone by.

Never bet your life on a gizmo. Dyson's lip curled in disgust as the Old Man's voice ran through his mind. *Gizmo's can fail.* No matter what new piece of tech Dyson tried to show him, the answer was always the same. *Stick with the basics, the basics won't let you down.*

"Yeah, yeah," Dyson muttered as he fired an airburst 20mm grenade over a stack of forklift pallets, the proximity warhead detonating as it flew over the makeshift barricade. More white splatter in IR. "Stick with the basics my ass."

The Bounty Hunter glanced at his chrono. Thirty seconds and still no sign of this Gort motherfucker. *How tough can it be to find the jolly-fucking-green giant?* They needed to move faster. Storming a large building like this was always a crapshoot that could go to shit in a heartbeat.

The no-knock warrant gave a bounty hunter a much-needed bit of edge. You could come in shooting and thin the bad guy herd before they knew the fight was on. Not very sporting, but critical to this kind of run. Cops could secure a perimeter, reduce the numbers inside to a finite calculation. They could seige, holding tight while the trapped offenders got tired or hungry, or maybe just stupid.

Bounty hunters had none of those weapons in their arsenal. Actions against gangs started with you being outnumbered and outgunned, and Bad Guys could call reinforcements.

A powerful jolt shook the building, strong enough to shake handtools off shelves. Zach's icon flared red on Dyson's HUD, then black.

What the fuck? Dyson broke into a hard foreward charge, blowing past a couple uncleared doors. "Sego," he snarled "you got this."

Sego started to say something about breaking formation when an unseen force knocked the wind from his lungs, the words abruptly lost in a percussive exhale. Over the comm Dyson heard the rapid pang of bullets tearing through graphite armor.

"Goddammit," Dyson cursed, hitting the brakes at the top of the stairs. Uncertainty tore at him, the muzzle of the carbine snapped down the stairwell, then back along the hallway through which he'd just run. "Sego, talk to me," he barked. "What the fuck's going on?"

The voice on the comm transitioned from pummeled fighter to a thick, wet gurgle as the drumroll rat-a-tat continued. Sego's icon flared orange, red, black.

"Sego!" he shouted, receiving no reply. "Connor, report." Barely a heartbeat passed before he added "Connor get the fuck up here." Dyson struggled to get the pieces straight in his mind. Sound was getting muddy as he fumbled to toggle the button that would spot-check the ammo in his carbine. Jäger used to talk about stress doing things to you: *tunnel vision, selective hearing, loss of fine motor—*

A shadow darted across the hallway and Dyson twitch-fired a burst, chewing a trail of holes through the synthrock sheeting. Bootsteps thudded behind him, no, below. Dyson rolled the railing and fired a burst down into the darkness.

"Fuck!" Connor's voice screamed out, the younger man throwing himself hard againts the wall to avoid the rain of tracers. "It's me dammit, it's me!"

Dyson blinked rapidly, horrified at how close he'd come to punching Connor's ticket. His eyes darted across the HUD. *Why didn't the— oh muther fucker!* The IFF, the system that was supposed to highlight friendlies from hostiles, had somehow toggled off. Dyson viciously rapped his helmet with his left hand, which accomplished nothing at all, before he took a breath and activated the subsystem. A green outline suddenly resolved around Connor in Augmented Reality, stark against the three or four red silhouettes forming up at the bottom of the stairs.

"Frag out!" Dyson shouted, one hand dropping the grenade while the other grabbed Connor by the front of his exo. Dyson threw himself backwards into a sprawl, Connor falling on top of him as the grenade went off. Chunks of building and occupant filled the air.

We're fucked, completely fucked. Dyson's mind struggled to regroup, ears ringing. Eighty-four seconds in and nothing but casualties on both sides. As he untangled himself from Connor and struggled to his feet he shouted:

"We gotta get the fuck outta here."

The two men staggered back up the hallway, into the foyer where a riddled Sego lay sprawled. The breacher's gun was gone, as was his sidearm. Dyson's non-stop stream of profanity paused as he keyed his mic.

"Lance, we're bugging out, coming your way. Shoot anything that gets between us and the door."

This had gone Charlie Foxtrot in a big way and Connor stared back with eyes gaped in fright. The weight of the last two minutes grabbed Dyson by the throat; Sego and Zack, guys that trusted his judgement, dead. Resolve coiled in Dyson's gut. *No more*. He grabbed the front of Connor's exo and leaned in, visor touching visor.

"Look at me Connor. Look at me!" The kid's eyes were twitching side to side, then swung forward and locked. Dyson stared hard, made sure the lights were on behind Connor's stare. "Look, we are out of here OK? Straight line, back to the ship then back to home. Stick with me and I promise I'll get you out of this."

Connor swallowed hard, then nodded.

"Good." Dyson stood, took a step through the front door, Connor rising on his heels. "Then let's get the fuck out of here."

"Hell yeah," Connor said. Then his head exploded.

Dyson looked through a visor splattered with brain matter. "Hold your fire, hold your goddamned fire!" The words tore from Dyson like a scream. "What the fuck Lance, I told you we were—"

The voice on the sniper's comm channel was deep, coarse. and unfamiliar... "Lance doesn't work here any more."

Dyson's gaze raced up the street, sliding up the tower when his right leg blew apart at the knee.

———

Jolted awake by the caustic burn of smelling salts, Dyson squinted up at the hulking silhouette. A deep gravel voice spoke with a odd, stilted pace.

"So my my boys tell me you come down here… to my place… an you make all dis' mess… lookin for me."

Dyson tried to rise but couldn't move, felt like he was glued to the floor. His eyes tracked to his left arm. *Not glued,* he realized. *Nailed.* A row of fifteen or twenty construction spikes punctured his arm from palm to bicep. It wasn't so much a scream that came out of him as a keening whine.

"Oh hey, hey, hey," Gort said, scrunching his face as though to the sound of fingernails on a blackboard. "Dat ain't how it's done. Have a little self-respect."

Dyson blinked, confused. "Wha–?"

Gort repeated himself great care. "Respect." As bizarre as it seemed, this Godzilla-sized thug was serious, enough so to explain. "Look at T over there. Muggs is pullin' frag outta T's face with, what the fuck is dat, needle-nose pliers? Yeah. Well you don't hear T goin' on like a whiney little bitch do ya?"

Dyson shook his head, more confused than ever. *Was he not about to die?*

"You guys," Gort grinned as he leaned forward, waggling a thick finger. "You fuckin guys, wit yer bounties and an your fancy-schmancy gadgets. Bad enough we gotta deal with the cops without you piss-ants tryin to make a quick buck off our ass."

As if struck by a distant memory, Gort slowly shook his melon-sized head. "Used to be you bounty guys had *stugotz*, big fuckin' balls. You made your bones, fought a man nose to nose, ya know? But now…" He reached a finger and flipped a shattered plate of carbon fiber off Dyson's chest. "What the fuck is all this? You knock off a toy store on the way here or somethin?"

A smatter of laughter came from around the room, an odd sound from the scarred, tatted figures who quickly fell back into a silent glare.

"Now dis, on the other hand," Gort stood once again to full height, hefting the breacher's gun in his hand. A two-handed weapon for most men, it fit Gort's oversized grasp like some kind of freakish, old-world flintlock. "Dis is nice. Dis is old school."

The smile drained from Gort's face. Whatever mirth there may have been in his eyes sank into a glower of burning coal as he leveled the muzzle at Dyson's face.

"Fuck the barbie-toys, kid. You wanna win a fight, stick to the basics."

IT'S NOT THE SIZE OF THE DOG IN THE FIGHT

The Slagheap, Brimstone

The German Shepherd circled left, favoring the bloody foreleg where flesh and fur hung off in wet strips. Half a dozen scars crossed her head and neck, one ear half-shredded. It snarled, eyes glaring, lips drawn back from a broken row of bared teeth.

The rust and black dog was lean, nothing compared to the weight of the mastiff. That thing was a Tibetan by all appearance, some freak mutant hybrid of dog and grizzly bear. Its fur was a cloak of dreadlocks matted with blood, mud and shit.

The mastiff roared in like a freight train, jaws driving for the shepherd's throat. The lighter dog side-stepped then darted in, chomping hard on a dark brown foreleg.

Howling, the mastiff drove forward despite the injury, knocking the shepherd off its feet. The bear-dog trampled the sprawled opponent, sinking fangs into an exposed upper thigh.

Using its weight to pin the smaller dog, the mastiff viciously marched its hold one shaking bite-width at a time, climbing toward the black and tan waist. The soft underbelly. The shepherd cried out over the roar of men and women waving cash, screaming "Kill, kill, kill."

A fight broke out among the two-legged animals massed around the ring. Things started to fly; fists, beer bottles, chairs. A half-empty bottle of Jack cartwheeled into the ring and smashed against the retaining wall. The mastiff flinched back from the sound, perhaps from the spray of glass, its shaggy head raised in alarm.

The shepherd twisted, lunged up, bloodstained teeth clamping shut on the exposed throat. Over 230psi of bite strength tore through muscle and crushed cartilage. The mastiff shuddered, eyes going unfocused as it buckled in a wheezing, convulsing heap. The humans shouted at the sight of death, their own brawl quickly forgotten in the wake of canine fatality.

"What da FUCK was dat?" Lazlo looked to be on the verge of aneurism, veins distended across his neck and forehead. Reaching up he grabbed Miller by the shirtfront and yanked him almost off his feet, stabbing a pudgy finger at the Shepherd. "It was supposed ta fucking die!"

Miller was an unkempt, balding piece of shit who ran the Brimstone dogfights. He fed Lazlo the over-and-under on each matchup, scripting the outcomes when the betting got rich. Precede a fight with a sedative, or one hell of a beating, and a favored dog ends up dead. Thats good book, good money for the house. Money for Miller.

But an unexpected loss, fuck – a loss like this was a disaster. The mastiff was a gold mine for fodder fights, entertaining little exhibitions like how long it takes that monster to kill a dozen or so of the cat-sized rats that infest Brimstone's gutters. Just blood theater really, but more important, it made a name that drew real challengers in from Leir 1-Alpha, sometimes as far as Mya. The fucking mastiff never lost.

Sweat running down his face, Miller looked at the mountain of fur twitching in a pool of red. *Well it bloody well lost now didn't it?*

Lazlo still hadn't stopped screaming, his anger turning to the crowd. "Get out, EVERYBODY get the fuck out!"

As though electrified, the mob dispersed across the slagheap as Yvgeny slipped a loop of rope around the mastiff's hind legs to drag the carcass out of the ring. Nobody bothered to check if it was still breathing. There were no vets on standby; a dog that couldn't walk out on its own became food for the rest.

The shepherd had flopped over, panting on the dirt floor, blood oozing from a dozen wounds. Its sad brown eyes looked around for anyone to lend a hand. Instead, Lazlo picked up a handful of garbage and threw it at the dog. Missing only made him angrier.

"You miserable fucking mutt." He cursed, stepping forward to hop the low wall and kick the dog to death when The Swede rounded the corner with Benny the Twitch in tow. Lazlo glared.

"What part," he growled, temper now past yelling, "of 'tell Gort to bring Welker' didn't you understand?"

The Swede wouldn't go out of his way to pick a fight with Lazlo, but he was one of the few people who worked in the outfit that didn't much give a shit about the little man's foul moods. Facts were facts and the shortest line between any two points was a Swede.

"Gort is cleaning up that mess at the chop shop." He spoke bluntly, the fact irrefutable. "Welker hasn't been seen for days, not since Brogan got back in town. That takes no imagination. No Gort, no Welker, so I bring you Welker's bitch."

Lazlo drew in a deep breath; the logic was sound but it did nothing to improve his mood. Nothin was going right but goddammit, he couldn't kill everybody.

That thought hung in his mind for a moment. Well, he could kill everybody, maybe, but if their replacements were drawn from this little shithole, they'd likely be just as fucking useless.

Focusing himself, Lazlo walked to Benny, who stood upright only because the Swede's hand was clamped around the back of his neck. A malnourished skeleton covered with the lesions of a Krok-addict, Benny nervously chewed what was left of a dirty fingernail.

Lazlo opened with a crushing slap, his usual introduction. "You know who I am?" he barked.

Benny shuddered like one of the beaten dogs, pawing confusedly at his split lower lip.

Lazlo hit him again. "Do you fuckin KNOW who I am??"

Benny nodded. The combination of frantic head-bobs, trembling and junkie twitch looked like the onset of convulsions.

"Good," Lazlo spat. His nose wrinkled as he looked Benny up and down, voice suddenly a glower. "You even think about shittin' on my floor and I'm mopping it up with your face. You got me?"

Benny nodded again, a nifty trick given the neck-clamp, but he pressed his knees together. Just in case.

"So listen up. Welker owed me information, only that little fuckwit is probably goo inside a cube of crushed steel by now. So his problem just became your problem."

Tracking less than half of that, Benny kept up with the nods, likely as not because thus far it had kept him from getting belted again.

"So whatta ya know about the Doc? What's he up to?"

Benny's face wrinkled, perplexed by a question he couldn't nod his way out of. He chewed another nail, his left hand scratching at a scab on the side of his neck. "Doc?"

Lazlo grabbed a fistful of Benny's hair and wrenched the scrawny neck from the Swede's grasp, dragging Benny face-first to a stack of cages. He shoved the junkie against the metal bars, the chained dog inside responding with a predictable mix of fear and anger. It lunged, teeth ripping a hunk out of Benny's tangled mop.

"He's been talking to Ed!!" Benny shrieked, grappling for any recent memory.

"Ed." Lazlo blinked. "Schizo Ed?"

"Yeah," Benny babbled, his face flecked with dog-spittle. "They been spending time in the Nek, hanging out with the Xi'An."

This time Lazlo scowled. "What the fuck they doin with the *reptiles*?"

Benny reached into his bag of knowledge, found it empty and started to cry. But before Lazlo could feed him to something furry and awful, a tiny spark flashed. "Sasha! Sasha said something about Ed brokering a deal for Doc. Something big."

Lazlo stopped, considering the words. Benny was a fuckin cockroach but roaches get overlooked, they hear things. Doc had been blowing off explaining the whole severed head thing.

Needed more time, Doc had said. *Doing science shit.*

The gangster fumed. Maybe Doc don't need no more time for science, maybe he knows what was stuffed inside that shmoe's melon and he's cutting a deal with the fuckin reptiles. Lazlo's rage flared. *Cuttin' me out.*

Lazlo yanked Benny face to face, ignoring the stench of rotted teeth that surpassed the reek of sweat and old piss. He viciously twisted a fistful of Benny's hair, jacking the kid up onto his toes.

"Now listen up fuckstick, and listen good. You are Doc's new shadow. Where he goes, who he talks to, if he takes a dump I wanna know where, you got me?"

Benny managed a weepy series of nods.

"You fuck this up, you run, you let Doc figure out you are watching him and so help me I will chop you into bloody little pieces and feed you to these fucking dogs."

Lazlo didn't need to wait for a reply. He shoved Benny towards the Swede. "So get the fuck outta here. And take a goddam bath ya filthy peasant."

The Swede ushered a weeping Benny out of sight, leaving Lazlo alone in the now-empty slagyard. "I swear to god if that fuckin little tweaker screws this up I really will feed him to—" Lazlo caught himself, his head snapping back to the arena.

The fucking dog.

Grumbling under his breath Lazlo pulled the pistol from his belt, too exhausted at this point to spend time kicking the animal to death. He walked to the low wall and swung the pistol over…

bare dirt.

A line of bloody pawprints led out the open gate.

A SHADOW IN THE DARKNESS

Kins II : The Calavaran Shelf

I am not death, for death is eternal stillness,
the unwaking sleep.
I am the sudden violence that precedes death,
the snap of bone and the rend of flesh.

~ Kage no hon
The Book of Shadows

She watched the shark glide silently past the 49th floor window. The dorsal fin alone rose almost two meters above the sleek grey back. Nose to tail the leviathan had to measure somewhere near twenty meters.

Kemuri admired it; every gram of its hundred ton weight existed for the sole purpose of killing. A faint smile tugged at her mouth. While she stood shorter than its fin, Kemuri had killed more people in the last thirteen minutes than the shark had likely killed all week. Corpses, stuffed in crannies across several floors of the tower, gave silent testament to her lethality.

Mindful of her schedule she crossed the room; an indistinct shadow ghosting across the huge glass window. Had anyone been watching she might have been taken for a momentary ripple in the shifting glimmer of light that made it down to this depth. Such was the benefit of active camouflage, the surface of her armor coated with electronic chromatophores patterned off the very octopi that slithered through the reef outside.

While not as powerful an illusion as the light-bending stealth armor favored by Special Forces, e-chrome was completely passive. Yes, remaining unseen demanded diligence on her part, on fluid motion and boundless patience. But unlike the soldiers with whom she sometimes worked, she didn't show up as a bipedal black hole on a spectrometer scan.

Killing was easy; killing unnoticed was an art.

Normally, travel from the surface down to the master suite was done via express elevator, but that was a road marked by redundant layers of guards and detection gear. Few would think to snake their way through five floors of air ducts to reach open stairs. As such, this floor, much like the sixty-two above it, remained largely empty and without lighting. Glowstrips ran the seams between floors and walls along the central pathways but normal illumination relied on flourescing panels that would activate when something living walked in.

But ghosts didn't trip sensors. Kemuri crossed the room in undisturbed darkness, offering neither footfall nor body heat to betray her presence. By altered genetics, by a lifetime of training and an unbreakable oath, Kemuri was *Ikiryō:* a wraith. The sleek, high-tech armor didn't hurt.

She would have preferred killing only her primary target, leaving witless minions to scratch their heads and spread fear of her kind. But her employer had other directives.

Just as well, she thought. This particular target had spent good money to surround himself with above-average minions, the kind that randomize their patrol routes and schedules to avoid being predictable. The kind that just as arbitrarily pair up to walk circuits normally executed by a solitary guard. The parts of two such figures were stacked in a utility closet up on the 63rd floor, her first contact coming down from the roof. That was the only part of the tower that extended above sea-level. With each floor she decended, the number of personnel, and the frequency of their appearance, dwindled.

She had her target to thank for that last fact. His abusive intolerance was almost as well-documented as his wealth. The son of Banu aristocracy, Zul-Ren came by his fortune the old fashioned way; he inherited it. This was not to say that he failed to display the bloodthirsty ruthlessness of his mother who had amplified the fortunes of her father before her, but Zul-Ren was a child of privilege; over-indulged, thin-skinned, just a hair-trigger away from a tantrum over the tiniest slight, real or imagined.

Ren was spiteful, corrosive, demeaning to anyone deemed beneath his social stature. It is one thing to fail to win friends or earn their loyalty, it's quite another to be so malignant that others will pay to see you dead.

Kemuri had a term for people like Zul-Ren: job security.

As a matter of *shibumi*, Kemuri rarely took pleasure from her work save for the quiet satisfaction that comes from flawless execution. But the more she learned about Zul-Ren in preparing for this contract, the more she felt she was doing the universe a public service.

Among Zul-Ren's many sensitivities was an oft-repeated complaint about being disturbed by the footfalls or door-opening of security personnel, or having to suffer from lights, floors above, filtering down into windows on the 40th floor. That was Zul-Ren's "personal space."

It seemed to Kemuri that the Banu man-child placed far too great a reliance on the unassailability of this aquatic fortress, as though the hefty price tag translated to real security. She could not imagine the cost of sealing and refurbishing a skyscraper that had submerged when the melting of polar ice caps flooded coastal cities up and down the continent. Kins II had become yet another planet from which the Banu largely packed up and left, abandoned now to slavers... and people like Zul.

Drawing on a myriad of microsensors in her armor, Kemuri saw a thermal silhouette through the door ahead. With two rapid steps she crossed the gap, grabbing the sword on her back as the door slid open.

From *tachi-ai*, the standing posture, she drew and struck with a single motion, a *tsuki* thrust that drove through the figure's throat before the door had fully opened. Wide eyes blinked with shock for just an instant before she rotated the blade ninety degrees, sharp edge left, and whipped it free, severing trachea, carotid artery and jugular vein.

Half-decapitated, spinal cord severed, the guard slid to the floor with a soft thud. Kemuri snapped a reflexive *chiburi*, flicking the blood from the blade before returning it to her back.

Along with the latest body, Kemuri disposed of the guard's ATT-4, still unfired by now-dead fingers. This was an age of starships and laser rifles where the sword was, by any logic, an impractical weapon. Its range was intimate, its mastery demanding years of sacrifice. It was dependent, without exception, on the strength, speed and skill of the wielder.

Yet these very qualities made it a tool like no other, both offense and defense, weapon and shield. It was silent and elegant, immune from a crippling addiction to batteries or ammunition. It was the weapon of choice for a ghost.

This particular sword adhered to a classic design. Shorter and thicker than a formal katana, the curved blade sacrificed reach for extraordinary cutting power and mobility in confined space. Qualities one might need to cleave through armor in the confines of a starship, or in a tower reclaimed by the sea.

Unike the mastercrafted blades of antiquity, this *chisa katana* was a doctoral thesis in material science. The nanocomposite blade wasn't hammer-folded, it was assembled one molcule at a time. Magnesium alloy, osmium-cored for mass, with a diamond-hard edge that only tungsten could deliver.

The ebony damascus finish inspired its name: *Kuro Hi.* Black fire. The monniker only hinted at it's thermal properties, as extensively engineered as the physical ones. Those were truly exceptional.

Kemuri decended the last set of stairs, arriving on the 40th floor. The doors ahead fit snugly as did all of the others, doors that as part of the retrofit of this building could act as watertight bulkheads should a window fail and the ocean rush in. She stared at the door, the sensors in her armor absorbing the rythmic throb of music playing softly beyond. Micro-changes in surface temperature suggested that lights were on. She studied the door closely; four heavy dead-bolts were seated into the frame. It appeared that the time for stealth was at an end.

Kuro Hi slid silently from its sheath as she squared herself to the door. The accelerators in her nervous system kicked in, the world around her slowing to a crawl. Her grasp on the handle tightened, a surge of power flowing from her armor through contacts in her gloves, crossing into the sword. The black damascus steel took on a dull cherry glow that quickly blazed with veins of orange incandescence. She drew the sword overhead and lunged in, striking with a force that split the door down the center.

At a dead run she burst through the gap, small launchers in her shoulderplates fanning pellets in her path. The tiny spheres burst into clouds of black smoke. She charged, e-chrome matching the broiling black so quickly that she looked like a viper made of smoke racing through the room.

The big robot deployed, both its existence and location predictable. Petulant though he may be, Zul-Ren wasn't an idiot and if living guards were not to be present in his inner sanctum, automated ones would be. That the 'mech was stored in a recess on the innermost wall was predictable as well. It would have weapons that were designed to pose no threat to the wall of glass, but one could not guess what an adversary might bring. Drawing fire away from that outer wall was just common sense.

Kemuri dove into a roll as the robot's twin guns belched out blobs of adhesive, most likely that military 'nano-glue' that actively spread itself across a target on contact before constricting like a python. The shots tracked high, drawn off-target by energetic particles in the smoke acting like chaff. She came out of the tumble, launching herself with a powerful stride up the side wall; a twisting leap that hung her in the air above the machine. Power surged and the katana blazed, arching down like a falling star.

A moment later Kemuri stood over the pile of smoking debris, sparks popping where severed edges of robot armor glowed orange-hot. She turned with a fluid grace, the long trail of smoke at last evanescing to reveal her true form.

Perhaps a bit dramatic, she conceded, but an indulgence she allowed herself.

Zul-Ren back-scrabbled across the floor, stabbing madly at what would most certainly be the Panic Button on a small remote.

Kemuri paused, turned her head to listen, then smiled behind her featureless facemask. To nobody's surprise, save perhaps Zul-Ren, no one left alive was rushing down to give their life in his defense. It appeared that the petulant little shit finally got the quiet he demanded.

As she walked slowly towards him, the sword burned with a fury.

YEAH, YOU CAN TELL HIM I SAID THAT...

HAB 42, Apartment 19, Brimstone

"Yeah I'm bloody well watching it right now." Darius griped at the voice on the Mobi while he tracked the center screen with maybe forty percent of his brain. The remainder of his attention was split among the four other panes of data that floated around the first. Multi-tasking, real no-shit parallel processing, was a gift Darius had enjoyed since childhood.

One of those screens displayed a scrolling cascade of information as a real-time decryption alogrithm chewed through INN's site-to-station firewall. That gave Darius invisible eyes on raw feeds before they were edited or streamed to the rest of the 'verse.

"How the fuck should I know?" Darius groused. "Some beat-to-shit dog just limped into the shot. They chased it off, and they're starting over." Air-tapping a series of holographic buttons he added, "Yeah, yeah, I'm pushing it to you now."

The INN logo flashed up on the screen, along with the usual QR code, timestamp and geolocation data. A slim, well-built man stood holding a microphone, silently mouthing his opening remarks. A voice came in from off-camera. "We are live in five, four, three…"

<BROADCAST> "This is INN news correspondent DeAndre Tate, standing at what many are calling the crossroads of tragedy. Behind me is the now-infamous Nekropilis, a burned-out section of industrial arcology Leir One Bravo. It was just over three years ago that this innocuous mining center, perched on the edge of space, found itself the front line of the growing war with the Vanduul. The numerous charred buildings and carbonized human figures throughout the Nek are a persistent reminder of how abruptly war can spill over its boundaries. A sense of outrage and abandonment is prevalent among Brimstonians, many of whom tell me—" </BROADCAST>

"Brimstonians?" Darius scoffed out loud, flecks of Guinness foam sputtering from his lips. "What the bloody hell is a fucking Brimstonian? No, I jus— Fine." He fell silent, allowing the transmission to continue without his color commentary.

<BROADCAST> "— leader of the Xi'An delegation, has refused to be interviewed, issuing only a terse statement that Xi'An presence here is focused exclusively on humantiarian efforts and the mitigation of any persistent health hazards that might stem from the thermoplasmic event. But the lingering impact of the as-yet unresolved Co'Ral incident, now almost two months ago, leaves many people wondering where UEE officials —" </BROADCAST>

"This is shite." Darius broke the feed, his agitated ADD jumping across to three other datapoints. "Any twat with half a brain knows it's all a bloody Agency front."

His fingers stopped in mid-air, brow furrowing as he listened to the voice in his ear. Darius responded, "You cannot be serious."

The hacker facepalmed as he listened to the reply, relieved that the voice on the Mobi couldn't see the gesture. "No– no sto– stop! Bloody hell mate, you're hurting my brain. Liste-- No, shut up and listen!"

He took a breath, thankful for the brief moment of silence. "Right. I'll make this simple and since it's you, I'll use small words. The news media is chocked full of intel spooks, full-up DES operatives running under various levels of cover."

Rapid-fire tones came from the Mobi for several moments before Darious spat back, "No, it makes *perfect* sense. They go everywhere, see everything. Nobody questions when they start filming shit, that's their bloody job. Oh here, step into the picture, maybe we can interview you. What did you say your name was…?"

Darius lit up another smoke, his ire growing the longer he listened. "Conspiracy theory?? How bout Occam's bloody razor? Given all possible explanations the… ah fuck it."

Grimacing, Darius groaned at the insufferable stupidity with which he had to deal on a daily basis. It would be easier to explain reality to the bloody dog on the telly.

"Here, here's an example." Darius said, suddenly seizing on a thought. "Stormy Winters, celebrated INN journalist. We all shed a tear when she damn near got her arse blown off a couple years back, having the damnably bad luck of getting an interview with Kintasa u-Buntu on the very day that UEE Special Forces rained a missile on his head. The story goes that it was only divine providence that saw her walk outside before the missile punched through the roof."

An interruption on the Mobi forced Darius to pause. His face reddened. "I know it was on live-stream dimwit, that's my point. She didn't 'just happen' to walk out in time, the bloody Reaper overhead was waiting for her to leave. Think about it. You have a high value target, maybe the supreme terrorist of the day. He's the bloody sod who killed off that other INN reporter on Bacchus. Nobody, not DES, not the Banu M23, nobody can get eyes on this guy. But he wants to get his message out, wants to publish his manifesto, so who walks in but Stormy Winters, interviewer of the stars."

Darius was on a roll, his energy building. He didn't give the voice on the Mobi a chance to break his stride. "It's the stuff of journalism legend. A reporter all alone, Daniel in the Lion's Den. Kintasa is no idiot, there's no way somebody sneaks in a bug or a transponder, only Stormy doesn't need one because the drone upstairs has her 5GL bioscan. From twenty thousand meters up it can pick her out of a crowd of thousands on the unique aspects of her neuroelectric signature. Don't you get it, she IS the beacon, she sets herself up as the target and parks herself in the same room as the Bad Man. It's bloody brilliant."

Darius shifted the smoke to his opposite hand, monolog running unbroken as he grabbed a drink. "Only the muppet flying the drone gets a little ancy-nancy on the trigger button and blows his load before she can get a safe distance away. Building gets leveled, Kintasa gets dead, but Winters gets injured. Ratings go thru the roof and Winters wins a Zelnik Award. You say it was some huge collection of coincidence? I say bollocks. Everything went damn near exactly as planned."

Darius paused at last, the next couple minutes rolling his eyes as he listened. At some point the veins on the side of his head started to pulse. "Believe what you want but—"

Darius paused, taking a long drag on the cigarette while squinting at the central screen. His tone softened. "Hell-low."

The voice in his ear rattled something but Darius gave it no more than five percent of his mental bandwidth. The rest of his capacity was focused on a waveform that played along the bottom of the screen. A signal inside a signal really, like a metallic thread invisibly woven through an intricate tapestry. His brow knit, fingers dancing across virtual screens.

The buzzing in his ear grew cranky.

"Shut yer gob for a bloody minnit willya?" Darius responded, his focus far away.

Squinting at the display, Darius peeled the layers of moving image and sound into separate streams, struggling to strip away artifacts interlaced between them. It was like trying to separate digital velcro. Then a scratchy, broken vid began to stutter in the second window. He leaned in and expanded it to full-screen.

It was an outside scene, maybe any one of a dozen industrial docks around Brimstone. Darius noted a row of heavy incinerators in the left background. His brain churned through mental references. Eastside then, third or fourth quad. That was Vane's turf. Darius narrowed his eyes and he leaned forward.

The camera was peering over a stack of crates, furtively looking at something large. A big-ass ship. Yeah, cargo bay open, lot of guys inside, standing at attention.

"What the fuck are they holding?" Darius muttered under his breath. "Flags?"

The stream broke apart into digital snow, an explosion of pixels that fuzzed the screen. Darius cursed, rapping virtual buttons in a flurry of motion. The pixel-storm cleared just as the camera zoomed in, the hand-held jerking now made worse by the extreme magnification. Darius upped his profanity to match the stress, but countered with a stabilization routine. The picture cropped down to a smaller bounding box but what remained inside settled dramatically.

Not flags, Darius realized with a start. More like poleaxes. Halberds. Bunch of guys in green armor with…

He felt his jaw go slack.

Bloody fucking hell, its them. They're here.

Darius spoke into the Mobi with a tone that did not invite challenge or question. "Get Lazlo, get him here. Now. No I'm not fucking sending you anything over the wire. Tell him to get his pint-sized ass down here right now, I think I know what Doc's been holding out and it ain't just the turtles involved in this thing."

Darius exhaled a lungful of smoke, eyes unblinking as he listened to the strident tones. "Yeah, you can tell him I said that."

I LOVE WHAT YOU'VE DONE WITH THE PLACE

Mine 3, The Nekropolis, Brimstone

As the elevator cleared the shaft and descended into the huge cavern, Ed said dryly. "As you can see, we've made some improvements."

I blinked several times, wondering if the image would suddenly give way to a more conservative reality. Ed had told me that the Xi'An made a lot of progress remodeling the lower levels of Mine 3. But this was…   words escaped me.

When I first saw this place it was little more than the original mine hub; a house-sized room carved out of the rock several hundred meters below ground. The floor had been littered with portable workstations, cobbled together in a spider web of cables.

Back then the 'science experiment' plunked in the center of the room was little more than a spherical Faraday cage;

curved emitters that struggled to maintain a tiny scale model of the thermoplasmic event. Pretty much a melon-sized plasma ball. The whole thing was dark and damp, held together with duct tape and baling wire.

My eyes swept the room as it stood now. "How did you…" I waved my hand in the direction of the sphere. "How did all this happen?"

Ed shrugged. "Don't ask me, it came out of your head." He gave me a sidelong glance and saw my confusion, then added. "Not the one you're wearing, dumbshit, the one from the workbench."

"Oh, yeah," I muttered, still soaking it all in. I'd been in air traffic control centers with less equipment. This wasn't a mine anymore, it might as well have been the heart of an Arc Reactor.

A huge shimmering globe dominated the center of the room. It looked like glass, maybe five meters across, filled with a persistent thermoplasmic reaction. Unlike the first experiment I'd seen, this wasn't some spindly ball of energy. This was robust, burning with a steady writhing fire.

I pointed at the globe. "That thing won't break, will it?"

For a moment Ed's eyes flared wide, as if the possibility had not been considered. "Fuck, I hope not. Shit that'd likely kill all of us."

He paused to watch the color drain from my face, sucking the lit end of the cig to a bright orange glow. Then he scowled and shook his head. "We're not stupid Doc; it's a force field, not glass."

Not that I felt comfortable around a living reminder of the worst night in my life to begin with, but the answer just prompted more concerns. "Well what if we lose power? What if the field comes unglued?" I pointed at the pulsing reaction, my tone rising in pitch. "Can that shit get out???"

"Of course it can," Ed growled, impatience in his voice as he flicked the spent butt and fished in his pockets for another. He lit it, took a drag and finally added "This little experiment won't work if we don't let it out."

I don't smoke, but I sure as hell had a sudden urge to drink. All I had to swallow was the spit in my throat and that suddenly ran dry.

"All right," I muttered without a shred of confidence, "let's get this over with." A line from an old movie played in the back of my brain. I should have taken the blue pill…

Despite my discomfort, Ed forced something of a grin clenched on the cig. His eyes had one of those multi-Ed color changes going on, the blue tone burning bright. He slapped me on the back, a hard smack that rattled my teeth. "That's the spirit," he chortled, then strode off towards a prominent control panel. "Not like any of us is gonna live forever anyway."

I really do need to kill him. The thought came unbidden. It's not like I'd ever kill Ed for real. Hurt him maybe, but I draw the line at killing friends. So far anyway. Keeping a wary eye on the shimmering globe, I trotted after him.

I must have been standing at the wide console for a minute or so before I realized that the nearest lab-coated technician was Kuang. No fancy robes, he looked like any other turtle-nerd in the room. The sudden recognition threw me into another momentary blink-fest before I stumbled for a greeting.

He waved off the formalities and went nose-down in a tablet, offering only a brief nod to acknowledge my presence. Like everybody else scattered around the room, Kuang was all business as he said "Increasing power to thirty-five percent."

"So what's gonna happen?" I prodded Ed.

"We're gonna tear off a scab." Ed's attention was already focused on the globe but he reached out and picked a pair of goggles off a rack. "Here," he said, shoving a pair in my direction, "put these on."

I slipped them on, more of an electronic scuba-mask than anything. The full-face front lens was not transparent at all, instead some sort of prismatic sensor panel. In darkness my fingers fumbled over the outside of the apparatus until I felt a hand take hold and depress something that clicked. With a sharp soft whine the room appeared like an out-of-whack 3D x-ray. My ability to see through objects ebbed and flowed, people around me drifting from silhouettes to walking skeletons with belt buckles, eyeglasses, a stainless steel hip joint...

A hand squeezed my shoulder; it was Ed. His skeleton was wearing goggles like mine but good god, what was going on behind them? For a moment I thought his brain was on fire. Then it hit me; the fireworks going on inside his skull was the rest of the Eds.

"Mind your own fucking business," he growled none too nicely, a brusque hand rotating my head back towards the globe. "Look over there and tell me what you see."

The light inside the globe was amplified a hundred-fold; I could see waves of energy pulsing out to bash against the inner surface of the force field. It suddenly looked less a force of nature than it did a living thing; angry, beating at the walls of its cage. A really bad taste bubbled up the back of my throat.

My rapt fixation on the globe began to subside and my mental camera pulled back, expanding my awareness of the room. Lab-coats moved to and fro, two of them walking towards the —

My heart seized in my chest. A massive forked rope of energy, vague and indistinct, extended out from the globe, out through the wall of the cavern. My breath caught in my throat, eyes darting to see a second leak, a third; wavering patterns of light that reached out from the same focal point. A figure stood next to one, some woman with a backpack. Even in the bizarre transparency I could see the fear etched into her face. One of the twisting arms wavered down from above her.

"LOOK OUT!" I shouted, tearing the goggles from my head.

The light show, at least any of it reaching outside the globe, disappeared as the goggles came off. So did the woman. Save for the hum of electronics, the room fell silent. Goggled faces turned in my direction.

"Xīn lái de jiāhuo!" Ed said loudly, punctuated with a dismissive wave. The herd of nerds turned back to their work. Ed on the other hand looked at me intently. "Tell me exactly what you saw."

"That fucking thing is leaking," I began, discovering how hard my heart was hammering. "It's like, spreading, all around…" I fumbled the description, words giving over to big hand gestures.

Ed nodded, his own gesture a rapid roll of 'move along'. "What else?"

My eyes darted back and forth, confusion rising in the midst of alarm. *Where the hell did she go?*

"A woman," I muttered, stepping up on a crate for a better vantage point. "Middle age, shoulder-length hair, had a backpack."

Ed closed his eyes for a moment. I could see that rapid-eye movement behind his lids, the REM-sleep reflex that happens when he taps the collective Ed-pool. The eyes snapped open, freakishly bright.

"Dierdra." Ed said, looking at Kuang, "that's a fourth for her." Kuang nodded, as if the comment had some deeper meaning.

I stared at Ed, wondring if I had taken an elevator into a mineshaft or into the Twilight Zone. Irritation started to compete with the other emotions running amuck in my brain, but I was remarkably calm when I asked "You gonna explain this to me?"

Ed peeled off his goggles. "Yeah, sorry 'bout that. It was important to get a natural reaction without planting suggestions in your mind." He motioned me to a chair and, truth be told, I was glad to flop into it. I wanted that drink even more.

"First off, it isn't leaking." Ed led off with what was, for me at least, the bottom line. "What you saw outside the globe are tears in space-time left behind by the original event. Call 'em scars in the fabric of our reality."

I'd be lying if I said I understood half of what that implied, but I nodded and listened.

"They are benign, for the most part, but they can tell us a lot about what happened that night, about where things went."

"Went?" My mind grappled with the word. Shit got fucked all to hell but not a lot went anywhere.

Ed glanced upwards for a moment. Maybe he was considering his next comment, maybe he was getting whispers from another Ed, I never really understood how that worked either. Whatever transpired, he looked back at me and continued.

"A whole lot moved Doc, in both directions, just not the way you'd normally think of movement. Let go of the idea of objects and imagine instead that half of the atoms in something swapped places with atoms from something else on the other side. Random replacement of the little lego blocks that everything is made of. So what was living flesh a moment ago is now some marbled swirl of flesh, petrified wood and volcanic glass. Same basic shape, only the composition is utterly different."

It sounded vaguely logical, and that fact on its own scared me, but the whole idea raised a million new questions that I sputtered in a jumble.

"But the woman? Where did-- and you said 'swapped.' Swapped with what?"

Ed gave me a reassuring pat on the shoulder. "Easy there cowboy, you'll sprain something. Now you are asking the big questions, like 'what's behind door number 1'. And just about..." he glanced up at an overhead console where a chrono burned above a matching countdown timer, "six days from now, we're gonna kick that door open and find out."

HELL OF A BREAK THERE DOC

The Claddagh Pub, Brimstone

Fitzsimmons barked, "Shut the fuck up Carl!"

As bartenders go, Fitz was a big bastard, well over seventeen stone and naught but a bit of that turned to fat by a few too many stouts. Truth be told he was a bit of an irish stereotype, a mix of red hair, pale skin and green eyes that were, at the present moment, burning with a fire. His fingers bunched around the bar towel in a big ham-sized fist.

Carl stiffened at the sound of his name. The more he strained to make the handle 'Slash' take hold, the less traction it got. Fitz knew Carl back when he was a scrawny, snot-nosed delinquent stealing hubcaps off PTVs, or whuffing gasket sealant in the back alley with the other little street rats. Carl was older now, but sure as hell no wiser.

Nonetheless, Carl turned slowly away from Tommy, struggling to throw his best 'I'm a badass' glare. At a spindly eleven stones for a meter-six in height, the results were laughable. Add the scraggly hair and a beard that looked more like the fuzz that grew wild on a man's ass, and Carl was more likely to be called 'trash' than 'slash'. Death metal tats up and down his arms, along with the black leather vest covered with biker patches, finished off the whole 'MC wannabe' persona.

Fitz glared, the muscles tightening down his right arm. He growled, "C'mon boyo. You take just one more step, givin' me that look, in my pub."

Now Carl was a lot of things, and none of them laudable, but he had that little light in the back of his brain that Mother Nature in her infinite wisdom granted to every lizard, rat and roach that crawled upon the earth or any other planet. It was the one lone bulb that signalled a creature, no matter how dim, when it was pissing up the food chain. Sometimes that bulb gets ignored; thats when things die horribly.

In this instance, Carl nervously glanced to either side and saw nothing but Fitz' regulars, most of whom were quietly hoping he was dumb enough to bluster just one more time. Few things were as entertaining on a Thursday night as a first-rate ass-whuppin.

To their collective disappointment, Carl slinked out the front door without a word, the silence broken by laughter and a hail of napkins, french fries and beer cans tossed at his back on the way.

Fitz grinned. Notwithstanding the likes of Carl, he had a great bunch of customers. Had it come to blows, with Carl or anyone else, Fitz'd not face the fight alone.

"Hooligans, all of ye," Fitz said with feigned grouse as he picked the bits of garbage up off the floor. The statement only drew more laughter.

With a pat on the shoulder Fitz muttered "Sorry about that Tommy" as he walked past the pool table on the way to the bar. Tommy shrugged an *'ain't nothin'* back and turned to line up his next shot.

Fitz paused at the pass-thru, holding the hinged section of bar up as Megan slid by, a platter of food in one hand and three frothing mugs in the other. He gave her a big grin, the kind you can muster when you are boss and father all at once. Megan flashed her blue eyes, her mother's eyes, dishing smart-ass comments left and right as she made he way between the tables.

She got that from her mother too, Fitz chuckled.

Having lapped through Fitz the Bouncer and Fitz the Dad, he cycled back to Fitz the Bartender and surveyed the room still thinking about a fight. He scanned the bar from left to right.

Jarlson was working his second beer; he'd be good for a fight if it came to it. O'Donnolley was drinking Jack straight, he'd be wanting another in the next couple of minutes. Fitz figured he'd be most likely to bite off somebody's ear in a good donnybrook.

Oksana was still in her welder's coveralls and throwing down vodka, which meant some guy was likely gonna get hurt later tonight. Fitz winced at the thought of the havoc she'd cause if given truly good reason.

Doc was at the end of the bar, nursing a scotch and a corned beef sandwich.

Well, there's Doc, Fitz thought. *Some are born fighters, some are fixers.*

Come to think of it though, Fitz noted, there probably wasn't too many folks in here that Doc hasn't stitched up at one point or another. If you're not a scrapper, a ton of good karma might be more useful than bullets.

Fitz gave a quiet sigh, enjoying the sound and smell of a local pub. The bar was solid and Megan had the tables in hand, including the back table half screened-off from view. The business table.

Vane had been holding court back there quite a bit lately. Fitz had no idea what the pirate was up to, in fact he made it his business not to know, but the stream of visitors were hard to ignore. Yakov came and went, Bridger, Hoskins, most of the usuals. Petrovich was an oddity, the fabricator not one you would peg as being a part of Charles Vane's social network, but it's a big 'verse. Draga, well, Fitz gave a slow whistle, *Draga could spend as much time in this bar as she likes.*

Fitz rolled that image in his mind for a long, dreamy moment, then glanced about nervously. *Well, as long as Megan's mother wasn't around.*

At precisely half past six MacGregor came through the front door, a study in graphite epoxy that spider-webbed across every front-facing centimeter of his clothing. Fitz waved him over to an empty stool, thumping a freshly-drawn Guinness down on the bar. MacGregor dropped onto the seat with equal thud.

"Yer a fine man Fitzsimmons, despite everything they say about you." The wiry figure picked up the mug, raised it to Fitz with a smile and in his thick scottish brogue added "Slàinte, ya mick bastard."

Fitz nodded and chuckled as he wiped the bar, the ritual a part of life in this pub for more years than he could remember. He grinned; MacGregor in a fight was reason to call paramedics. Maybe a Cutlass full.

Without any ado MacGregor began his circuit. "Doc, ya wanker, here's at ya!" From the far end of the bar Doc looked up from a tablet, mouth stuffed full of half-eaten sandwich, and waved for a moment before grabbing his scotch and returning the toast.

MacGregor made his way around his circle, offering his usual curses of endearment till he hit the bottom of the mug. In his usual fashion, he looked up at Fitz as the replacement hit the bar, then asked the usual question. "So Barkeep, what's the news of the night?"

Fitz dutifully ran through matters great and small, a discussion that ranged from goings-on at the back table to finish on kicking Carl out of the bar.

"Ah well that explains it." MacGregor said, Guinness-froth on his moustache.

Fitz cocked an eyebrow, prompting MacGregor to elaborate.

"Ah the cuntybuggeryfucktoleybumshite is out in the alley throwing rocks at a poor rag of a dog."

To the best Fitz knew, that rolling string of names was about the worst thing a Scot can call somebody. He turned, as did O'Donnolley, and looked out the window.

"Awww no." Sure enough, that beat-to-hell mutt that has been laying up behind the dumpster was now backed against the wall. Carl blocked the alley entrance, throwing whatever rocks or bottles he could find. Fitz felt his ire rise.

Why you little piece of...

Motion caught Fitz' eye as Doc stood up, shoved the uneaten half of his sandwich in a coat pocket and started for the door. Fitz sputtered, "Doc, you want me to wrap that up—" but was waved off.

Doc stopped halfway past Tommy, turned back and said "S'cuse me a sec." and gently took the pool cue from Tommy's hand. Tommy looked at Fitz with a confused shrug as Doc walked out the door.

The bar pretty much fell silent as Doc crossed the street and without so much as a 'how-do-you-fucking-do' smashed Carl in the side of the melon with a Babe Ruth swing that sent teeth and wood splinters heading over the outfield wall. The crack – definitely wood, maybe bone – echoed through the bar. Everybody winced as Carl dropped like a sack of shit, face down in the garbage.

Doc looked down the ally, pulling the sandwich out of his pocket as he took a slow step forward. It was too far for Fitz to hear but the dog hunkered down and showed a half set of teeth. Doc stopped, took a slow knee, then set the sandwich on the ground and backed out.

It was dead quiet in the bar when Doc walked back in, handing the splintered half of a cue-stick back to Tommy. He plodded to his seat, fished a twenty out of his pocket and slapped it on the bar, muttering "for the stick."

Fitz wasn't sure what to think. He didn't give a shit about the cue, he was dying to ask *who are you and what the hell did you do with Doc?'*

On habit Fitz swept the bar with his eyes, noting the slack-jawed customers. The only one who didn't gape was Charles Vane, watching from the back of the room. Vane looked at Doc intently, a dark smile crossing his face.

"Jesus, Mary and Joseph," MacGregor chuckled, breaking the silence as he lifted the mug to his lips. He paused, then burst out with a foam-splitting laugh.

"Hell of a break you got there Doc."

ZOMBIE-13, AIR SUPPORT IS INBOUND

Gonn, Oberon System

Another Gorgon slammed into the dome. A hemispheric pattern of hex facets shimmered in the air when the warhead went off. The force field soaked up most of the frag but a surge of heat and overpressure rocked the Marines inside.

"Last pack out!" Lampley shouted, jacking the orange handle to eject a spent powercell and seat the last fresh one in its place. The force field emitter thrummed and the sound of battle dulled. Lampley looked at the display and patted the device. "She's good for two, maybe three more hits max."

"SITREP!" Dragon barked, her eyes towards danger. As a MARSOC Gunnery Sergeant, Emi "Dragon" Comoto had a rep for keeping a cool head when the shit hit the fan. At the moment, surrounded by at least a hundred Vanduul, the entire fan was submerged in shit. The rotating blades were just stirring the brown stuff.

The responses came rolling in. "Badger good." "Mercer, good to go." "Lampley, Kyle and Scones, all good."

Dragon tracked the shout-outs to the translucent icons spread across her HUD. She didn't expect an answer from Yeltzin; chunks of him were dripping down what remained of the left-side wall. That left just one unaccounted for.

"Jansen," she barked. Half a breath wait, then "JANSEN!!"

A wet cough came from Dragon's far right. "Yo" The voice was muddled.

Still tracking enemy movements with her carbine she reached back, snapped her fingers and pointed forcefully in Jansen's direction. "Get eyes on Jansen."

Kyle scrambled over rubble and slid in beside the seated heavy weaps specialist, diving into a rapid assessment. It took only a moment. "Shit Gunny, he took some frag."

"How bad?" she asked, ducking reflexively as the crimson finger of a beam laser scraped across the dome. She expected Kyle's typical smart-ass dismissiveness, a product of the medic's well-earned confidence. As a rule, if the head is attached, Kyle figures he can get it home still blinking. The silence tore her gaze off the front line.

Jansen was seated, the front plate of his armor rocked open where Kyle was forcing a thermal coagulant into one of three notable entry wounds. Blood bubbled out of the other two, a bright red froth that came out in gouts each time Jansen's chest settled. Comoto winced. *Lung wounds.*

"Crystal Palace," she shouted into the comms, "this is Zombie 13 actual, we are bandicoot, I repeat, we are bandicoot. Where the hell is our air support?"

"Don't get your panties in a knot, Dragon." Even over radio static the voice was warm, laced with a familiar southern drawl.

Comoto's eyes flared. "Luce, you son of a bitch, tell me you're here." For the first moment since this shit-show fell apart, she felt a glimmer of hope.

The voice came back. "Roger that Zombie-13, The Fallen are three mikes out, rolling hot. Looks like you threw a real party down there."

Another Vanduul missile shrieked in from the old factory down the street; a solid hit. The dome shuddered, overpressure hammering Comoto's ears and chest. She scanned the ruins that surrounded her Marine's position, every corner layered with Vanduul crew-served weapons, shoulder-fired missiles, mortars. It seemed like every dark crevice blossomed with muzzle flare.

"They're right on top of us," she shouted, a hint of scream tainting her voice.

"That's why command cared enough to send the very best darlin." Then Lucifer's voice lost any hint of humor. "Keep your head down Dragon, we're about to fuck some shit up."

Dragon spun to her troops, palms mashing towards the ground. "GET DOWN!!"

The air outside the dome ripped in half as a fan of hypersonic missiles screamed in, low and flat. The Gorgon launcher disappeared, along with eight or nine other heavy weapons. A wave of Hellstorms followed, belching submunitions that skipped across the broken pavement like oversized ping-pong balls before bursting white-hot. The heat washed over what was left of the dome, scorching metal just outside the field.

Thunder shook the ground as the Fallen screamed by, barely twenty meters off the deck. The shockwave that raced behind them peeled asphalt off the roadway.

Comoto looked up, her eyes tracking the carnage. The primary Vanduul crew-served weapons were now tangles of burning metal. The AT-88 had been blown completely off the roof of the parking garage, now smashed and burning in the adjacent alley.

A garage-style door rolled up and an ad hoc vehicle lumbered out into the street. The commercial flatbed truck carried a fixed-base missile launcher. She barked into the comm "Technical, vector two-four-five!!"

The drawl responded, "Well shoot the damn thing Marine, what the hell good are ya?" The mirth was back, a soft chuckle just before the comm clicked off.

Goddamn right, Dragon snarled under her breath. *This was our fight to begin with.* "Marines!" she shouted, "My target, now!"

On her mark Lampley cut the dome and the Marines unleashed hell. Small arms fire raked the vehicle and launcher. The windshield dissolved in a cloud of glass, blood and brain matter, none of which was human in origin.

Driverless, the truck rumbled forward until its nose crunched into the side of the service center. Three of the eight missiles screamed off the rack, one venting flame from half a dozen holes along its length. It spiraled into the sky and detonated. The other two scorched off in search of loitering angels.

In response, one of the chameleon fighters color-shifted from ambient blue to blaze orange, as visible as it could be against a backdrop of tan dirt and grey sky. The missiles locked on, wheeling over at almost right-angles to give chase.

True to its name, the Fallen plummeted from the sky, yanking nose-up at the last moment in a burst of jet-thrust and countermeasures. The jet screamed skyward, fading back to shades of blue as the two missiles, lost and confused, slammed into the parking garage. The multi-floor structure collapsed in a roar of pancaked concrete.

———————

The lights in the room snapped on and Colonel Charles "Hammer" Martell set the remote on the podium. Mnemonic Recordings made After-Action Reports more vivid and detailed than any collection of narrated video or 3D animation. The men and women around the table were breathing hard, some visibly rattled. Politicians, even senior command staff, can live a lifetime without experiencing a cutting-edge SF engagement firsthand. The M-REC cut through all the bullshit. He could tell by the unblinking eyes that he had only to close with authority.

"Total engagement time one minute thirty-seven seconds. Five over five performance, bad guys dead, good guys come home." Martell looked around the table where UEE brass was flanked by Xi'An and Banu counterparts. The turtles were understandably invested, it was their shit that got stolen.

The Banu were less than thrilled; they'd been trusted with the package. When something gets stolen on your watch its a matter of honor to get it back yourself. If the Empire steps in and pulls out a win in the fourth quarter, the Banu look even worse. That weakens them, gives us leverage with the Xi'An we can work for decades.

He looked around the room. *Who would have thought that a platoon of antique statues could pay off in modern-day political clout?*

The probability of mission failure was low; the enemy was a criminal enterprise not some fanatic zealots looking to die for the cause. These clowns were in it for the money, used to dealing with cops who lacked Special Forces training, hardware and the authority to engage. These pirates, thieves, whatever their name or whatever rock they crawled out from under, were about to get a lesson in shock and awe.

"I'd like to turn this briefing over to Major Frank 'Lucifer' Hawkins, commander of The Fallen. He will explain to you how how the unique capabilities of his team will handle the situation. Major?"

Hawkins stood with a nod of deference to Martell. He picked the remote off the podium and tapped a button. The screen lit up with the image of a sleek, shark-like fighter.

"The Aegic Dynamics Saber…"

IGOR, THROW THE SWITCH

Mine 3, The Nekropolis, Brimstone

Let those who search for monsters beware,
for when you look long into the abyss,
the abyss looks into you.
~ Nietzsche

"Zàicì wèn wǒ, nǐ jiù sǐ dìngle." < *Ask me one more time and you're a dead man.* >

His eyes burning a freakish amber, Ed shouted at me in gutteral Xi'An above the pulsing thrum, the bass so deafening that it shook the stone walls. He had been working non-stop for five days; with no time to blow off steam his personality was shifting on the fly. I wondered if, in his present state, Ed still shared my hardline aversion to killing friends, or for that matter if I was still among that group at all.

Truth be told, I knew this whole thing wasn't safe, knew that nobody in the room had any idea what was about to happen. We were prying open places where the laws of nature had been broken. *Tearing off the scab*, Ed had called it. Who knew what the hell we'd find under the skin.

"Ninety percent." Tsun barked. One of Kuang's senior technicians, the lanky Xi'an was glued to the display, calling out power levels every few seconds. "Containment stable."

That last part was important, at least we hoped so, and I understood now the choice of a force field over a physical shell. The idea was to open the globe and let the beast peek out, but at the first sign of trouble, raise the field and close the cage door. Given what the first thermoplasmic event did, I was a little unclear on what a good outcome might look like versus a bad one.

"Ninety five."

I squinted at the globe; the energy inside was burning so brightly that it had become pure incandescence, at least through the goggles. There were more ghosts as well, although Ed would bite my face off any time I used that term.

Myoelectric echoes, residual neural imprints. Call me old fashioned but when a see-through image of a dead guy starts wandering around, it's a fucking ghost.

"One hundred percent." Tsun first looked at Kuang as he yelled the words, then at Ed. I couldn't tell if the wide-eyed expression was scientific amazement or raw terror. But the seismic shuddering now bled off of the walls and into the floor, the tremors running up my legs.

"Throw the switch." Ed yelled at me.

I had one job… and I couldn't help myself; it just came out. "Are you sure?"

Mayhem flared in Ed's eyes, so I closed mine and threw the switch. I don't really know if it did anything at all. Something in the back of my mind said it was a dummy, some meaningless widget put there so I could believe I had a part to play with no way to fuck things up. But with my help or in spite of it, the globe dissolved.

The feeling hit me before my brain registered the explosion of plasma tendrils. It was That Night all over again and puke bubbled up in the back of my throat. Fear rode the nausea, the whole mess becoming a PTSD train wreck. I grabbed the sides of the workstation, sucking for breath.

Bullwhips of energy snapped in all directions, but they really ran wild stretching up along the tears in the atmosphere. Tendrils overlapped one another, coiling thicker as they drove their way deeper into the crevices. Stray brances of light fanned out like roots seeking water.

A mob of figures staggered out of the core. At first they seemed like the same oblivious phantasms that we'd observed on numerous occasions, ghosties that gazed sightlessly as if in a fog. But these were aware; they saw the cavern, saw the equipment… saw us. Five, eight, a dozen plodded out, turning to the closest living person with a frantic wave, hands passing through coatfronts as they tried to grasp a lapel. Others just scrambled away from the light show, arms thrown high over faces etched with fear.

A stocky figure stepped through the tear and while I couldn't see his face - even looking through the transparency of his skull - he seemed familiar. Construction worker, could have been one of the numerous factory roughnecks that worked City Center before it got hit. The ubiquitous steel-toed boots, his belt ornamented with a knife or tool. The ghost looked left, then stopped, turning to me. I saw the look on its face when we locked eyes.

"Dutch." the name slipped from my lips, lost in the howl of noise.

Dutch, or whatever was left of him, stared at me. His eyebrows rose, head tilted in confusion, but I saw his mouth form a one-word question: "Doc?" It was all I could do to nod. Dutch took a hesitant step in my direction, then two, breaking into a run with his hands outstretched. I could see him cross the event horizon of the, oh hell, the *phenomena*. Thats where he disintegrated, dissolved into pixels that vanished in the air. I felt the cry ripped from my core.

The effect continued to grow as other things continued to fall out through the widening cracks. A car bumper, the door-panel of a washing machine, a street sign. That's when we saw the demon, or at least its ghost.

It stood taller than a man, muscled and long-limbed. Its hands were distended claws, talons that looked like they could open a throat without much effort. Eyes, deep-set in the extended skull, burned like hot coals over jaws defined by teeth and tusks.

A hand clamped on my bicep, a rough grasp that shook me on the edge of violence. I looked at Ed, his free hand pointed not at what emerged from the rift, but at the rift itself.

What had been a misshapen blob of energy had cracked open, pried apart by the tension of tendrils woven outward, tendrils that pulled at the center. I had the sense of looking down a long bending hallway, or more down a moving train where the doors between cars are propped open. What was on the other side seemed to sway erratically, connected in part to our world yet immune to one another's physics. Consoles and workstations filled the space on the other side, equipment that looked an awful lot like the shit in this room.

More demonic forms were seated among the various stations on the far side of the swinging tunnel. These did not appear insubstantial as the ones that had previously crossed over. They looked as real as Ed or I, as concrete as someone in the next room. Despite their horrific appearance, it was pretty clear they were as shocked to see us as we were to see them.

Ed spun to face me, screaming something I couldn't hear, jabbing a finger downward at the switch; at my switch.

I didn't need to ask, didn't hesitate. I punched that sucker like my life depended on it.

The containment field sprang to life, a geodesic jar of light materializing in the air. It sheared tentacles off the event, severed glowing appendages that quickly evanesced. Our ghostly visitors, human and otherwise, disintegrated as well. The bubble sealed shut, cutting the howl as well as the heat and light. The cavern room fell into silence save the beeping of machines and the lingering cries of terror and prayer.

I may have been the first to find my voice, but the question that fell from my lips was one shared by everyone in the room.

"What… the hell… was that?"

Tsun stepped forward, looking down at a piece of debris that lay smoking on the floor. It looked like the rotor disk from a turbofan. Whatever it was, it had not faded into ether when the door closed. It was real.

Ed walked towards the globe, pacing slowly around it, eyes fixated into its depths as the reaction faded to dullness. His foot hit something on the floor that skidded with a metal scrape. He stopped, bent down and lifted what looked like a… I blinked, squinted. A sword?

It was a wicked design, a sweeping razor etched with alien runes. Ed turned the weapon slowly in his hands. When he looked up, I could see a storm in his eyes, the color shifting in real time.

"This," he muttered, gesturing across the cavern with the blade as his numerous minds assembled the pieces. "That Night. It wasn't an attack." He looked up, his gaze meeting mine. "It was an experiment."

He stepped closer and placed the sword on the console.

"That wasn't some door to hell, it was a door into Vanduul space. They're trying to create a wormhole."

THERE'S ALWAYS PLAN B

The Claddagh Pub, Brimstone

Vane watched the stranger move through the bar, saw the subtle changes of posture that minimized human contact while slipping through a crowd. Using the back of the hand instead of the palm to move someone out of the way without their feeling they'd been pushed. That was training, and not the kind you get at charm school.

He was average height, nondescript to an extent that could only be by design. No obvious scars, no ink, even his eyes were a lifeless tone that fell somewhere between brown and grey. The kind of guy most people wouldn't notice; fewer still would remember.

As the stranger reached the back table, Yakov nodded towards a chair. The figure stepped past the offered seat, the one shoved half-out from the table, choosing instead the one that placed more of his back towards solid wall.

Yakov made the introductions. "Captain Vane, this is Halloran. He represents Mr. Smith." Everyone nodded, knowing that not a single name mentioned was given at birth. The fictions we maintain.

Vane's living eye never moved, but a blue prosthetic glow burned where the other eye had been. That eye told him a lot of things. While dressed like any other roughneck in the bar, the stranger was one of the only ones sporting a ballistic vest underneath, a high-end gelpack by the looks of it. Compact beamer under the left armpit, two blades pocketed snug against the ribs on either side.

"I'll give you the name of my tailor if you're interested." Halloran's voice had an edge of intolerance.

A faint smile tugged at Vane's mouth. *Observant as well.* The pirate dispensed with the pretense of sociability and settled down to business.

"Cash transaction, four million UEC in platinum or osmium bars. Cargo will be on a non-descript ship bearing registry of your choice, with enough range to get wherever you want to go. We meet, inspect cargos, swap keys and we both go our merry little way."

Halloran sat quietly, as if waiting for Vane to continue. After several long seconds he spoke, his tone laced with a hint of condescension. "The price is two million, delivery is a warehouse at Idris and nobody is flying a shipload of cash anywhere."

Looking down, Halloran tapped his fingers on a strip of holo on the table that seemed to have magically appeared an instant before the gesture. "Six interlinked GBA prime bank accounts. The money will be spread between them in uneven distribution. You can withdraw as much or as little from any given account, up to the full balance across all accounts," his brown furrowed, "but I wouldn't recommend that, larger withdrawls garner unwanted attention." He slid the holo across the table. "We verify the cargo, you verify the funds. What you do with it after that is your business."

Vane glanced down at the strip of holographic plastic. Six blocks of data, usernames, passwords, CORPSEC codes, amounts. At the bottom right a total appeared. Two million.

Hm, Vane gave a small chuckle, the sound a wolf might make when it sniffed a tidbit that could be food. Then his eye rose slowly to meet the pair across the table. "Three five."

Halloran sat for a moment, then pushed his chair back from the table. "Unfortunate. I suppose you'll have to find another buyer." Without a gesture, the balances on the holo spun down to zero.

"There are no other buyers," Vane replied.

Halloran paused, head tilted slightly as his brow narrowed again. Vane suppressed the twinge of amusement. *He wasn't expecting that.*

"I don't see how that works in your favor." The statement lacked Halloran's prior confidence.

Vane shrugged. "It doesn't. In fact the longer I have to keep the cargo in storage, the greater the likelihood that somebody will find it." The pirate spoke with neither threat nor bravado, but fell into an unusual eloquence. "I never set out to acquire something so… unique, a venture accomplished at considerable cost. And while it would be good business to recover on those expenses, it would not to the point of putting everything else at risk; my ships, my men. This leaves me, however regrettably, with Plan B."

"Which entails?" Halloran's attention was rapt.

"Cut my losses, push the cargo into a star and act like it never happened."

The response came quickly, gut-reflex. "Are you out of your mind? You're talking an irreplaceable piece of history."

Vane didn't blink. "I don't see how that works in *your* favor."

There are times when thermal is a useful spectrum. In infrared you can spot a man in absolute dark, follow footprints on concrete for a brief bit of time. You can also see when a man flushes, no matter what his level of self-control. Blood vessels up the side of the neck dialate and the heat flows. Thats why a very sensitive IR sensor was a part of Vane's left eye. He watched the dark bolus of spit slither down Halloran's throat.

"You wouldn't." Halloran posed it as a statement, but meant it as a question.

It was Vane's turn to be impassive. "Without batting an eye. These are rocks to me. I can sell them or be done with them, but either way my exposure ends."

Vane watched as Halloran's eyes shifted down and left, the barest hint of movement across his brow. Kinesthetic neural response, the kind associated with sensory perception. That and with lying. Vane held back the smile. Halloran wasn't the only one to have received some very special training.

Listen to your master boy, Vane thought with a passing wish to bare his fangs. He didn't need thermal vision to know that Halloran was wired, connected by some neural implant to Smith, who had been listening and directing from afar. Their eyes met and held, each trying to scry truth in those round windows to the soul. Halloran flinched first, speaking aloud, but not to Vane. "Yes sir, I do."

His gaze finally broke away from Vane's, dropping to the holo on the table. Vane didn't bother looking down; Yakov's intake of breath told him everything he needed to know. Instead, Vane's stare remained locked on Halloran as he slid his own document across the table. Not a fancy holoprint, but it would do.

Halloran picked up the sheet and read it thoroughly. He flipped it over, confirmed that the back was blank, then folded the sheet twice and slid it into his jacket pocket.

"You're serious." Another question masked in a statement.

Vane allowed himself a dark smile. "I'm always serious." Then the smile vanished, replaced with an icy succinctness. "Is that going to be a problem?"

Halloran sat for a long moment, but Vane would bet that it was in private thought and not discussion with the voices in his head. Halloran took a deep breath and exhaled. "No. Do you have a… designee?"

Vane was deadpan. "Working on that. I'll get back to you."

Halloran stood, his attention lingering on Vane. "I take it then that our discussion is concluded?"

For the first time Vane grinned as he extended his hand. "If you mean do we have a deal, then yes. We do."

Halloran took his hand, a firm grasp, and glanced down at the untouched holo, certain that Vane had yet to look at it. He chuffed, shaking his head as he walked away.

Vane watched him go, tossing a nod to Fitz who passed it along to the bouncers at the door. They stepped back, allowing Halloran to pass without impediment.

Yakov stared silently at Vane as the pirate picked the holostrip off the tabletop. The sum of three point five million burned in the bottom right corner. Vane stuffed the strip in his shirt pocket and slapped the Russian on the shoulder. "We've got work to do."

THAT'LL LEAVE A MARK

A Nameless Back Alley, Brimstone

Cold dark. Stars. Specks of light on black space. Wobbling, night sky underwater, wavering, blurred. Floating up– pain, no no no. Dark, crawl back into dark. Still. Don't move. Just stop breathing.

Voices echoed in the darkness, angry curses that slowed the rate at which the blows fell. Blurred faces, just fragments now, like broken teeth.

"–ow who you're fuckin with?" THUD.

"–what was in the brain, Doc?" CRACK. *That was ribs. Can't breathe, air knocked out, sides full of splinters. Ribs, yeah ribs.*

Then he was alone, drifting in and out of oblivion. Doc felt the cold suck the life from him, drain the feeling from his limbs; from his core. Cramps tore through his thighs. Sinking through an endless black expanse of frozen glass, he felt – sensed – something beyond the numbness. Something warm, pressed against him. Soft. No words, just the dull steady throb of another heart. He leaned into the warm.

—————

"Wha–?" I spluttered, light stabbing into my eye. Nausea, headache, everything-ache. It hurt to move, hurt to breathe. But I wasn't frozen, not that gut-cramping cold like before. My fingers twitched through a curve of fur. Through warm. It took forever for my vision to clear.

Brown eyes, two circles of mahogany that stared at me with an unspoken sadness. The big ears drooped to either side, framing a snout criss-crossed with scars. The dog was sprawled flat on the pavement.

That's when it hit me: so was I.

"Hey." I muttered, "Issh you." My words slurred, a fat lip and missing teeth conspiring to give me a thick, wet lisp. I ran my tongue across the jagged remnants of dental work. "Aw, thit."

The dog looked like I felt. My fingertips began to wander across her side where ribs were easy to find under skin that hung slack. Ridges stretched beneath the fur, rows of old bite wounds or beatings left to heal on their own. She took a deep breath and sighed. The sound carried the weight of a weary, lonely soul.

I tugged gently and she rolled onto one side where her head could rest in the hollow between my chest and tricep. I softly scratched behind her ear, her wounds so numerous that I didn't want to tear something open. She sighed again, a grunty sound. A wide wet tongue slid out and rolled across her nose. She was missing teeth as well.

I don't know how long we lay there, two punching bags sprawled in the garbage. At some point it became clear that help wasn't coming. If anyone had seen either of us, we'd likely have been discounted as among the dead.

It took a long time to drag myself upright, discovering along the way that several fingers on my left hand were broken. I couldn't guess how many ribs were cracked and hoped that no jagged ends were sawing their way into my lungs. I vomited once on my trek to sitting upright, rolling my head away from the dog as my guts heaved. If she could smell it, among the collective stench of garbage, piss and Brimstone, she didn't let on.

The drainpipe helped me cover the last move to standing up. Neither of my legs seemed broken, but a screaming pain in my back warned of a bruised, if not ruptured kidney. Sure enough, the red stain that ran down my pantsleg suggested I'd been pissing blood while unconscious.

I braced myself between the dumpster and the pipe, waiting for the world to stop swaying. The memories of last night were still muddy, but the pieces had already begun to fall into place.

Lazlo, that fucking little bastard.

I chided myself for blowing him off to the extent that I had, for getting lost in the Xi'An science fair experiment. I should have known the little shit's patience would run out, and that the repercussions would be awful. He'd stuck that little ratfuck Benny on my tail, a tweaker that ran with Digby, Welker and Carl.

Hm, I grunted. *Should'a hit Carl harder.*

Terrified that a facelong fall would put me back at square one, I hand-walked along the alley wall, matching each shuffled step with a right-hand grip on something. Step, grab. Lean, shuffle. One more brief round with the dry heaves and I reached the mouth of the alley. I paused, breathing in air that at least was moving. I looked down, then turned back.

The dog remained on the ground. I would have thought those eyes were as sad as they could be before, until I saw in them the onset of abandonment. Her ears, her very frame seemed to sag further into the pavement.

"Whar're you waiting for," I slurred. Her ears picked up as I beckoned with my busted flipper. "C'mon. Lesh go home."

With a groan of her own the dog rose, limping badly on one mangled foreleg. She walked up to me, her face a mix of fear and hope. We plodded off towards my HAB, two beaten, bloody souls without a full set of teeth between us.

The hike took a couple hours; it felt like a couple days. Of all the people I know, of all the people I've stitched together, not a one crossed our path.

I get it. Lazlo puts the blackball on me and anybody offering a hand is likely to end up in the same alley. I made it a point to avoid Fitz's pub, knowing damn well the guys in there would come out no matter who they pissed off. But they didn't need this shit, this was my problem to resolve.

I reached my front door and it slid open, proof that the RFID in my arm really can take a licking and keep on ticking. I looked down at the dog who stood shivering as she peered inside.

"You're home," I mumbled and she responded with a faint wag of her tail, then stepped cautiously inside.

I plodded to my office, at least that's what I called the unofficial little clinic where I routinely patch up the odd bullet hole, knife wound, whatever mangling was inflicted on the local criminal element. I loaded up two infusers, a general low-grade anesthetic and a metabolic accelerator. One to kill pain, the other to speed up healing. Then I turned; as much as I wanted to feel that blanket-warmth of a ketamine haze, I had a debt to repay.

"Pfffsst". I tried to whistle but only managed to bubble spit between puffy lips. I headed back towards the front room, passing a mirror on the way. I looked; that wasn't a good idea. The face that gaped back was misshapen, one eye swollen shut. My skin was a patchwork of color, angry reds and purples giving way in places to that sickly yellow-

175

green. I drew back my lips, split as well as fat, and counted the missing teeth.

Fuck, I thought wearily. *Those'll need replacing.*

There was a lot I could do with accelerated healing but some parts just didn't grow back. I'd have a new set of aftermarket parts to add to my collection by the time this was over. Petrovich had a slew of 3D printers at the fab shop; he could run out dental ceramic as easily as metal and stone. Looks like I'll be bringing him some more business. I thought about the dog and the new teeth she'd need as well.

At least we'll match.

I went into the front room, grabbing a bottle of single malt as I went by the cabinet. If the dog gets first shot at the drugs, I'm calling dibbs on the alcohol. I clamped the bottle against my body with my gimped left arm, using my right hand to pry off the cork. I knew that the scotch would feel like jet fuel in a busted mouth, I just never thought it would be flaming jet fuel. Part of me wanted to scream but the other part sucked down a long gulp.

"Hey, dog." There was no response, although I wasn't sure what I expected. I looked under the tables, under the desk, figuring she'd picked some dark corner to hide. Thats when I heard the sound. Snoring, a low rumble that rose and fell. I followed the sleep-sounds to find the dog was sprawled across my bed in all her muddy, bloody, shit-stained glory. Her muzzle lay square across my pillow.

I shook my head, wincing at the cracks in my lips as an unconscious grin tugged at them.

You did make yourself at home, didn't you?

I leaned over, stroked her fur, felt her body unconsciously lean into my touch. She didn't budge as the infusers hissed, first one and then the second. She would sleep now, a deep healing sleep. I pulled the side of the blanket up and over her and crept out of the room.

Alone, I tended to my own wounds. Re-setting broken fingers did nothing for my mood. Against all printed labels and manufacturer warnings, I mixed prescriptions and alcohol until the bottle ran dry.

As dawn's faint glow crept through the skylight I sat back on the couch, a Frankenstein patchwork of bandages, staples, dermaglue and tape. I closed my eyes, left hand shoved into the portable AUGMED, and sighed, feeling the slow steady throb of healing energy.

There were few things in life I would have told you I knew for a fact. The events in the mineshaft, the idea of artificial wormholes, threatened some of the basic science I'd believed since high school.

But there was one thing I knew, as certain as night follows day.

I was going to kill Lazlo.

RISE OF THE FALLEN

Oberon Sector
Bengal Carrier *SS Billy Shaw*

Lucifer paced around the holographic display, his brow furrowed. A translucent rendition of the sweeping T-shaped Merchantman hung in the center, surrounded by a private asteroid-belt of wreckage. Five swept-back Sabers formed a spherical perimeter; engines pointed in, guns pointed out.

Lieutenant Nathan 'Tombstone' Earp set his tablet down with a sigh. "How many ways you wanna go over this, Major? We've run it at low-intensity, high-intensity, total surprise and total awareness. These guys are criminals in homebuilts. They're cannon fodder and we're flying the cannons." He stood, rotating his torso to stretch a stiff back. "Any way you run the sim, we kick their ass."

Lucifer glanced up, the warmth of their friendship tempered by a hard, steel-grey stare from beneath that brow as he flicked an index-finger at the Merchantman.

"Thats what they thought to begin with."

His eyes snapped back to the Merchant vessel. *So how did they take you?*

The Banu had been both slow and slim on details. Either they really had no idea what took place or refused to admit they'd done a shit job of planning; neither of which looked good in front of their Xi'An customers.

It was pretty clear they had taken a low-profile approach, moving the cargo on a single ship rather than in a small fleet. Escorts draw attention. But the Merchant ship wasn't exactly stock, in fact they'd bolted some custom turrets in places the ship was never designed to support. Lucifer wondered if, at the onset of a fight when everyone went to trigger, they didn't just blow the circuit breakers and go dark.

Go dark. The words scratched at his brain. *No, not a bunch of pirates. Then again…*

Lucifer snapped into motion; he lost the drawl when he was serious. "Wex, give me a four by four grid on the debris field where the Merchantman disappeared."

The Sergeant, having faded into a slump, jerked upright, a reflexive "Aye sir!" off his tongue as he spun up the display.

A huge volume of empty space rezzed into holographic view, littered with the bits and pieces of ships left behind after a firefight. Other small icons dotted the vast black.

Lucifer scanned the map for tiny details. A faint smile tugged at the corner of his mouth.

You.

"Pull up the maintenance records for Comm Array Two Seven Niner."

The young Sergeant shook his head. "CA Maintenance data isn't in our system sir, NSA keeps that stuff locked… under…" He slowed, then paused, watching as his team leader cocked up one eyebrow. Abruptly Wex went nose down, fingers tapping rapidly. "Rog that sir, hacking NSA."

Lucifer suppressed a mild chuckle as he imagined some disgruntled mid-level manager at the NSA throwing a hissy about Special Forces getting into their shit again. Hacking into secure nets were part of the mission profile around here; nobody said it would always be an enemy network.

If you didn't want us breaking rules, you shouldn'ta taught us how to do it.

Columns of data silently spilled down a virtual plane in the air. "Good to go sir," Wex announced with unabashed smugness. "What are we looking for?"

"Component-level failures attributed to ESD. You won't find 'em on the mains; we already know the bad guys were busy flipping the breakers before moving into an area. Focus on the small stuff, attitude control systems, navlocks, shit that runs autonomically even when the Array is powered down."

Several seconds passed before Wex looked up, eyebrows raised. "Sonofabitch Major, how'd you peg that? Two Seven Niner blows not one but three navlock mods, all listed as 'severe electrostatic discharge'. MTBF of 19,000 hours per unit; odds of all three blowing at once are…"

Wex looked up at the ceiling as he rolled math in his head, then shook it off. "Pffft. Too low for my brain to figure. One in a billion? Or is it ten billion?"

Lucifer allowed his grin a moment's liberty. Then the smile faded as he looked back at the map, imagining chess pieces on the board. *You sneaky mother fuckers…*

Sensing the quandry around the room, he explained.

"EMP. The pirates set off a pulse. Fried the Merchant, but also scorched the Comm Array. The question is, how?"

As team weapons specialist, Tombstone took his cue. "Baby nuke, something like a M54. Maybe a Flux Comp, something they cobbled together out of scrap? Either way, that's a one-shot act. There's no reloading an EPFCG."

Lucifer nodded thoughtfully, then sensing the lull prompted, "Or…?"

Tombstone wrinkled his face. "What, a Sentinel? I don't see where these guys come up with a ship of the line. Somebody would'a noticed one of those gone missing, yeah?"

The Major stroked his chin. "A Sentinel yeah, but what about something older, something that looks like a whole lot of other boats out there." Their eyes were still blank when he said "What about a Warlock?"

He watched the dismissive scoffs that ran around the room and grimaced. Sometimes being the best, having the best at your fingertips, dulls your appreciation for yesterday's tech.

The space penguin hadn't been a player in frontline warfare for longer than most of these kids have been alive, but was a day not that long ago that hardcore SF missions snaked along on Avengers. Those were old school, with big class-5 GAU-18s on the nose instead of the anemic 3s they bolt on these days. Back in the day an Avenger could ass-rape a ship twice its size in a one-on-one; in groups the black-n-white deltas were like piranha.

"OK, homework. Everybody in this room is gonna become experts on the Aegic Dynamics Avenger. Flight ops, performance envelope, variants. Most notably, the Warlock EMP variant. Tomb, I want min/max on output, what it could do stock, how far you could beef it up today. One of those suckers comes smoking in and some of us could end up riding surfboards out there."

Lucifer looked at chrono on his Mobi. "Regroup in two hours. Wex, Update the sim to add a Warlock to OPFOR assets."

Wex was already typing. "Rog that Major, for which scenario?"

Lucifer gave him a scalding glance. "All of them." He clapped his hands. "C'mon Fallen, this is how we earn our wings." He barked loudly "You think training is hard??"

"Try losing!!" Every voice in the room chimed in; tired, frazzled, but all shouted as one.

"Damn right." Lucifer watched as his team scrambled out of the room. He stood silent for a moment, then turned to one of the black-mirrored windows that lined the briefing center.

"What do you think sir?"

The black glass slid down into the wall, revealing the shadowed room beyond, the row of chairs, and Charles Martell. The dark flat-top had all but given over to grey, making the gem-blue eyes seem even brighter.

Martell had a voice like gravel. "I'll have Hanson run the traps on any Warlocks, but a shitload of them have been decommissioned over the years. They're supposed to be de-MIL'd, but most chop-shops do a half-ass job on slagging the cores. One out of five probably end up on the black market."

The Old Man looked at Lucifer. "Good catch."

The senior Fallen nodded. "Banu intel was supposed to be working backtrack on where these statues might'a gone, or who might be behind it all. Anything come of that, or just more of their usual jerking around?"

Martell shook his head. "Fucking useless. They want this to go away but don't want us to be the ones that unfuck it." His eyes tracked rapidly side to side; Lucifer knew the Old Man was surfing his Mobi. "Looks like there is some unsourced data suggesting Leir may be involved, but they haven't released any analysis."

It was Lucifer's turn to sneer. "Goddamn Outsiders. Wouldn't that just be the icing on the cake? Makes sense tho, lot less Empire presence in that little parking lot. We need to beef up containment there?"

Martell chuffed. "Like the man says, 'its a big damn sky.' We've been re-inforcing the jump points and known trafficking routes, adding random patrols to sift the commercial traffic. But everything is borrow from Peter to pay Paul. Assets we pull for this clusterfuck are coming off the Vanduul line. We picked up three more TDYs this morning, the *Sumner*, the *Archer* and the *Davenport*."

Lucifer stared at the map, adding those bits of data to his personal Operational Picture. "The *Archer*, that's Scanlon's boat isn't it?"

IT WAS A DARK AND STORMY NIGHT

Salvage Yard, Brimstone

"Not a good time Doc."   Vane shouted over the pouring rain as he motioned the maglev to cross the open field. It whined forward, hauling two flatbeds piled with scrap to the waiting leviathan. A massive hydraulic arm was crumpling the bullet-riddled nose of a Hornet and stuffing it into the gaping maw, the crunch of steel mixed with the rumble of thunder.

"Make the time." Doc shouted back, taking a decided step into the pirate's personal space.

Vane looked him up and down, recent events forcing him to check that Doc wasn't holding a pool cue. He appeared unarmed, but decidedly amped. Vane's eye slowly rose to look the man in the face, then he turned and walked across the scrapyard to a half-open conex. Doc followed on his heels.

As Vane entered and pulled the metal door in with a squeal, a dog slipped through the gap. It shook a cloud of water before parking itself next to Doc, eyes fixed on the pirate.

Vane eyed the dog, then Doc. "Didn't figure you for a pet owner."

Doc waved it off. "Long story."

Thankfully, Doc didn't offer to tell it; Vane didn't have the time to listen. The growl in his voice was sincere as he prompted, "All right, you have my attention."

Doc didn't balk. "Lazlo and his boys had a long chat with me the little while back. The kind of chat that involves wrenches." Doc edged forward, seemingly intent on keeping the pirate's gaze. "He was under the impression that you and I were working together. Any idea where he got that notion?"

Vane's poker-face flickered with genuine surprise, along with a growing edge of irritation. He was willing to cut Doc a bit of slack for trying on his new-found pair of balls, but this 'getting in my face' thing was about to become unhealthy. Vane matched Doc's forward step with a bigger one of his own, bringing himself nose to nose with the medic.

"What did he tell you? Exactly."

As if feeling left out of the party the dog edged forward as well, her lips twitching to the rumble of a low growl. The tips of perfect white teeth glimmered against her black snout.

This was normally the point where Vane's ill-temper showed itself, but looking at the dog, tired amusement somehow pushed its way past his irritation. The pirate slowly shook his head.

Neither one of these knuckleheads have any idea who they are playing tough with.

Vane looked at them both; for the last couple weeks you didn't see one without the other and judging from his expression, Doc had become rather smug about his new bodyguard. Admittedly, the mutt had made quite a comeback, from a fur-wrapped skeleton to some 40 kilos of recovering muscle and brand new teeth.

Vane stared at the dog for several seconds, then took a knee and reached out his hand. The shepherd eyed him for a heartbeat, then edged foreward and lifted her head under Vane's fingers. Doc went slack-jawed at the sight of the most dread pirate in half a dozen sectors ruffling a dog's fur, muttering softly in its ear.

Vane looked up, saw the confusion in Doc's expression. With a faintly wicked smile he said, "It's a predator thing."

As he rubbed fingers through her fur Vane looked at the dog, noting some scars that would likely never go away completely. The pirate had plenty of those as well. A stormcloud passed across his good eye as he looked up at Doc's face, where tinges of purple and green still lingered.

"So what did Lazlo say, exactly?" Vane's voice wasn't threatening, but very firm.

Doc swallowed hard, took a slow step back and walked through his memories of that night. Getting jumped by a handful of Lazlo's goons, hauled to one of the usual warehouse locations. The warm-up beating, just to set the stage. Then the questions. What is Vane up to? He mentioned some news footage showing a very high-profile cargo on a ship here in Brimstone, a ship being worked by men loyal to Vane.

Doc skipped over the questions about Ed, or Lazlo's belief that the three of them were somehow in cahoots.

"So what did you tell him?"

Doc's face turned a shade of red. "Tell him? There is nothing to tell! Hell you tell me what's going on."

For a moment Vane appeared angry. There was a simmering in his voice that bordered on violence. "You're sticking your nose into things Doc, into places it doesn't belong."

But before Doc could reply the pirate raised his hand, motioning him to silence. "You've done right by me in the past Doc, stitched me up, taken care of my crew."

Vane stepped towards the doorway and stared out into the rain as the giant claw crumpled the severed wing of an Avenger like tinfoil. A growing pile of compressed metal cubes, each about three meters square, surrounded the ship. Workmen with cutting torches labored in the rain.

"I'm sorry you got hurt," Vane continued, his volume lower but the tone no less feral. "If you're thinking I had a hand in that, that I set you up, the answer is no. But I promise you this," Vane turned, visible anger burning just beneath the surface. "I will settle this account."

Doc gave him a long look. For just an instant Vane thought he would speak but Doc caught hiself, nodded and simply walked out into the rain. The dog dashed after him. Vane watched as the two of them disappeared into the night.

Walking back into the deluge, Vane plodded across the muddy tarmac. He stepped over pieces of scrap, taking a moment to watch Sully spot-weld jagged bits of sheet-metal across a seam that ran up one of the cubes. He slapped the beefy figure on the back as he went by, the only response a brief bob of the welder's mask.

A swept triangle of white lay angled on a heap of parts. Vane shouted at Breslin to make sure the second wing went into the shredder with the first. Breslin dropped the chainsaw and pulled out a radio, looking up at the windows in the Reclaimer. He motioned towards the wing and the big claw reached out with a whine.

The pirate finished his circuit of the yard, mentally adjusting timetables as he punched up a number on the Mobi. Two soft beeps, then the Russian's dark voice.

Vane growled. "Yeah its me. Call the buyer and tell him we have a name."

CRY HAVOC AND LET SLIP THE DOGS OF WAR

Banshee System

Engines off, cold as ice, the five Sabers hurtled through space at blistering speed. They were flying IFR, the canopy bubbles chroma-shifted to be a black every bit as opaque as the ship's skin.

Lucifer looked at the dots on the HUD. A Banu Merchantman crept along the event horizon of Banshee, surrounded by a dozen smaller ships. The cleverness of the pirates continued to impress. Banshee was a pulsar, belching out far more electromagnetic energy than a normal dwarf star. It was dense, the mass adding to its powerful gravity. Hugging the edge of that gravity well cut the pirate's exposure down by almost half. It struck him that in another life, the captain of this crew might have been SF material.

"Fallen this is Fallen One, contact in thirty." He glanced at the RCR system, the small hex-shapd icon glowing green.

Rapid Combat Restart would be critical coming out of ghost mode in the next twenty-eight seconds. A green icon on his HUD indicated that somewhere aft, small remote camera drones were ready to deploy. Eyes and ears for the fleet that was parked safely out of sight.

Grudgingly, Lucifer had to hand it to the Banu in small part. Late to the game with little to show, their intel guys broke some SIGINT traffic that tipped the move. Turned out the Leir angle was right. Comms pinpointed some little jerkwater colony in Outsider space called Brimstone. They even knew the key player.

Lucifer chuckled. That end of the deal was cop business, although he doubted the Feds stood a prayer of showing up before the tidal wave of hungry bounty hunters. Regardless of who won the race, whatever scumbag was behind all this was about to have a very bad day.

"Contact in ten, hot in six."

The five Sabers were synchronized, allowing fly-by-wire links to manage precision moves in 3D space at speeds beyond human comprehension. Even with neurochems juicing his perception, this fight was gonna play out fast.

"Remember, this is a seize mission, so don't shoot the big boat. Hot in three, two, one."

In a flash of a network pulse, the five Fallen angels came to life. Canopies state-shifted to crystal clear, HUD data splashing over a live look into space. The RCRs cut loose, force-feeding voltage through systems that sprang to life. Engines roared, shields blazed ready, and missiles fired.

They had selected initial targets using passive sensors, taking advantage of a tiny flaw in the pirate's plan. The pulsar's glare could play hell with active sensors but it basically backlit the ships sneaking past it. Initial missile-lock focused on black tears in the blue radiance.

The instant the Fallen uncloaked, missiles streaked off their rails, closing to targets at hypervelocity speeds. The fight became formal when a light grey Merlin vaporized into a ball of burning fragments. Another detonation ripped the wing off a Hornet.

Lucifer scanned for a specific target, active sensors now picking shapes that had overlapped in passive silhouette. An Avenger hung low beneath the Merchantman's belly, too close to the target to risk a missile shot.

"Fallen Two, aft. Three, suppression fire on the Banu ship. Just scrape the turrets off. Four and Five, thin the herd." From the looks of things, Three had the easy day; most of the Banu turret guns registered as powerless. The damage it suffered during capture must have been irreparable.

Lucifer pinned the Avenger, watching as the HUD produced trailing-lead PIPs calibrated to his various weapons. His loadout was all kinetic, four Gatling guns on fixed mounts for maximum punch. He rolled in on the Avenger and fired.

The PGU-13 rounds slammed home along the twin dorsal intakes, shredding fuselage all the way up to the curved canopy. The force of the fire drove her into a port roll, belly rising up in a cloud of debris and vented gas.

Lucifer was already cycling his next target when he hurtled past the dead EMP ship, a silent snarl on his lips.

Pulse that, motherfucker.

Targets across the HUD were winking out as the Fallen cut through them like wolves through sheep. Fleet was staged just out of sensor range, EMS and support ships at the ready, but this was already looking like a rout.

To his starboard, countermeasures sprayed from Fallen Four and Lucifer spotted a Mustang diving down from above. He worked the HOTAS and pedals in a single reflex, unencumbered by the restrictions of COMSTAB flight. The Saber snapped sideways to travel and fired, filling the Mustang's flight path with four streams of high-explosive incendiaries.

Despite their adherence at selective fire, the Banu boat was suffering collateral injury. Some piece of wayward ordinance must have slammed into her midships, setting off a string of secondaries moving aft. Hull plates bowed out and peeled away, vomiting debris and cargo into space. Bodies tumbled into the void, frozen in stark attention. *Frozen like statues.*

A curse came across the open channel. "If I go down, we all go down."

Before Lucifer could process the improbable threat, another voice shouted.

It was Fallen Three. "EMP cycling up!"

Lucifer blinked, unable to comprehend what appeared outside his canopy. Blue lightning crackled outward from the Banu ship, brilliant forked branches spilling out through the gaping hull wound.

Lucifer's eyes flashed back to the shot-up Avenger, its slow barrel roll of death bringing the un-zipped spine back into view. Between shredded sheetmetal and split bulkheads were half a dozen criminal containment units, nothing more.

Lucifer's gut twisted. *Wrong Avenger.*

Time slowed to a crawl as his gaze snapped back to the Merchantman, to the lightning that poured from her hold. His nose-cam at max zoom, Lucifer peered inside where the Warlock Avenger, its wings, nose and tail cut away, had been shoved inside the Merchantman's belly. Then everything went white.

———-

Lucifer blinked rapidly, trying to clear his vision. Though the Saber's beefy engines were knocked offline, the cockpit wasn't quiet. System tones and alarms chimed haphazardly in every direction as systems stunned by the EMP struggled to reboot. Some displays shrugged off the hit, others wobbled in confusion. His sensor array was working, weapons offline, engines re-cycling.

Sumbitch! Lucifer cursed, his southern roots showing in anger. *Had he just a few extra seconds warning he could have powered down, mitigated the impact of the pulse.*

An alarm pinged from his sensors as dots lit up along the length of the Merchantman where turrets were suddenly powering up.

Not dead, Lucifer realized with a gut-twisting suddenness. *Just held offline till the EMP shot off.*

He looked out of his canopy and saw Fallen Three floating dead in space as half a dozen turret guns swung to bear. Lucifer banged on his comm, screaming "THREE GET OUT!!"

The Banu guns fired, streaks of light converging on the explosion that had been Fallen Three. Fighter parts shot off in all directions, none larger than the ejection pod just a step ahead of the blast. It tumbled through space, falling, Lucifer realized, down into the star.

Falling, he realized with abrupt horror, *like the rest of us.*

Waging war on the edge of a star's gravity well is one thing when you have engines, but deprived of thrust everything starts to accelerate towards the fiery blue globe. Lucifer cursed, fingers flying across controls as he barked out a Mayday. His engine sputtered for a moment, then died again. He looked at the Merchantman, a space-faring

Titanic whose stone passengers drifted from her breached hull. History looked to repeat itself as—-

Something exploded just above his canopy. A thundering concussion hit as a red blur shot by as if fired from a gun. Lucifer craned his neck to track the huge projectile when his own engines roared to life. The HUD still sputtered but he could run basic flight ops with his eyes closed.

Lucifer barked across the comm: "Fallen, sound off!"

Two, Four and Five called out, each in similar states. Lucifer looked for Three, for the lifepod beacon. There was nothing. The proximity warning droned. They were on the outer edge of the star's event horizon, in a few seconds it would be impossible to pull away.

"Fallen RTB, priority one!" He held his throttle as he watched one, two then three thrust-trails streak away from the crippled ship.

The Merchantman's black hull tumbled silently down into the sea of burning plasma, the crush of gravity already beginning to crumple her steel. Lucifer tried to imagine the Captain on board, and hoped that he was still alive for the last screaming ride to hell.

THE VULTURES ARE CIRCLING

Banshee System
Idris-M Frigate *SS James Archer*

Scanlon watched the battle live-stream on SecNet. As things came unglued and ships started plummeting into stars, he was reminded why it was he liked being posted as a glorified bouncer watching the outside door. For what it lacked in high-speed, low-drag decorations on a dress uniform, it more than made up with job security. Follow the rules and things work out with very few surprises.

"Sir, we're being hailed. Commercial vessel at 4800 klicks."

Scanlon's head snapped around. *Well that's a surprise.*

He looked at the HUD splayed across the front of the bridge. Archer was patrolling the Orange Zone, the void between the inner Red Zone where the battle was being fought, and the outermost Blue Zone where the Davenport was supposed to vector off any wayward civilians.

Scanlon looked at Colter, "ID?"

Colter was quick with the answer. "Reclaimer sir, flagged out of Idris sector. Regs are current and—"

"Brogan." Scanlon face-palmed, waving Colter to silence with the other hand. "What the hell does he want?"

Colter looked up from his console, confusion etched on his face. "He's declaring an SOS Captain, but, isn't that a ship full of mechanics?"

"SOS my ass." Scanlon grumbled. "If he's broken down I'll eat my hat. What's his status?"

"Engines off, lights on, doors unlocked sir." Colter said with a shrug. "Aside from being inside a secure perimeter, I'd give it a Two."

Scanlon nodded. A Two was the functional bottom of the scale; there was no such thing as a One. If you didn't find anything at all, you weren't looking. There's always something.

Given his 'druthers right now Scanlon would send Brogan on his way with a verbal boot up his ass. Still, the ship would likely be showing up on fleet scans, most certainly once it started hailing on an open channel. If Scanlon jumped on it quickly enough, the only career-shitstain that was likely to stick would be on Isky in the Davenport. That was reason enough to go.

Scanlon pointed at the blip on the HUD. "Let's go pay him a visit."

The airlock door groaned open and Scanlon walked aboard the *Goliath*. Jake Brogan and his crew all sat in plain view. No weapons, no surprises.

Scanlon grunted. *At least somebody out here still remembers the rules.*

Scanlon walked up to Brogan as the Illicit Traffic Search Team began a cursory sweep. Lefkowitz, senior Sergeant on the ITST, glanced at Jake who none-too-discreetly held up a hand with three fingers.

"What the hell are you doing out here Brogan?" Scanlon interrupted. He really wasn't pissed, if anything the interdiction was a break from listening to a fight go all to shit.

Jake motioned Scanlon to walk with him, strolling aft while the search moved forward. Jake rolled into a story that Scanlon hoped would not be long.

"So I'm working a dead Orion that looks like a rock blew up in its face. We're just peeling the skinplates when Isky rolls in on the *Davenport* and gives me the boot." Jake grimaced. "When did that schmuck get promoted to Captain anyway?"

Scanlon gave him a sideways glance. "You don't wanna hear about it."

"Yeah, well I'm guessing it involved knee pads," Jake grumbled. "Whatever. So dickhead sends me packing one way, sorta urgent like, which tells me something interesting is going on in the other direction."

"So you figure you come and take a look."

Jake held up his hands. "C'mon, he just chased me off from paying work that took me a week to find. You can't blame a guy for wanting to recover. Look at this shit." He opened a heavy steel door that led to a shallow balcony overlooking the compactor chamber. A huge set of grinders hung from the ceiling, shredder-blades decorated with streamers of metal and wire.

Far below, compressed cubes of scrap metal barely filled the lower third of the monstrous hold. A stench rolled up the metal cavern; a mix of petrochems, caustics, reactor coolant and bilge systems. Just about every sort of liquid that pumps through the veins of a starship mixed into 'starship soup.'

Nose wrinkled, Jake waved at the smell while Scanlon gagged out, "Augh jeeze, close the fucking door already."

The door banged shut with a slam and Jake picked up without skipping a beat. "So I figure, if you guys are stomping the crap outta somebody, maybe that somebody pushes a Nine and you need a ship chewed up."

Jake glanced to either side before adding, "I'll cut you in, straight-up share, all cash."

Scanlon suppressed a derisive laugh. "I wish." He offered nothing more.

Jake continued to probe. "C'mon, no… drug dealers? Slavers? Scumbag arms merchants who—"

"Stow it Jake," Scanlon was sharp, maybe more than he needed to be. But there was a lot of brass in this part of space right now and he didn't need some junk-jockey trying to wheel and deal inside a secure perimeter.

"Look, this is above your pay grade so I want you to ass-end this thing and get out of here. Pronto."

Jake held his gaze for a long second, hanging onto a thread of hope. Scanlon wasn't budging.

Jake sighed. "All right."

As they turned back Jake tossed a thumb back at the compactor door. "You're not in the market for some scrap are ya? Go 22-8 a key and they're yours right now."

Scanlon was growing weary of the wrangling and gave Jake what his crew referred to as 'the hairy eyeball.' Jake's shoulders slumped in final defeat. The two men plodded back to the airlock in silence.

The Search Team was standing idle by the airlock door, Lefkowitz more interested in Jesse's ass than watching out for his boss. When Corporal Pearson stiffened up with a muffled cough, Lefkowitz spun-to and pointed at the crate on the deck.

"Sir," he sputtered before collecting himself. "No VBT sir, but uh, on a thorough examination of the ship we discovered a small crate of contraband stashed away in… "

Jake, arms folded across his chest, wiggled three fingers over his bicep.

Lefkowitz rolled his eyes. "section 3. It appears to be Elysian Bourbon. No big deal but it doesn't have transit stamps."

Like a bad actor on opening night, Jake offered a mockery of excuse. "I have no idea how that got there."

Scanlon snorted. "Then I suppose we'll have to confiscate it," he announced dryly. "I presume we can let them off with a warning, Sergeant?"

Lefkowitz nodded. "Yessir." Then he hefted the crate and followed the team into the airlock.

Jake turned to Scanlon and tossed a nod towards the crate. "It's not much, things are tight." The scrapper offered a tired smile. "But you gotta find something if the Big Brass out here is breathing down your neck. There's no such thing as a One, right?."

Scanlon smiled in spite of himself. Though he'd never admit it publicly, life would be a lot easier with a few more Jake Brogan's around. To be sure, Scanlon had no false illusions that Jake was some sort of Boy Scout, far from it. Odds were he was as crooked as anybody scraping an existence off the rocks out here. But he didn't go out of his way to be a dick, to make things difficult. He understood the rules.

"Where you headed?"

Jake shrugged. "Don't much care, hate to go home on an empty belly but things are looking pretty slim and its clear we outstayed our welcome." He exhaled wearily. "I doubt that load'll cover the fuel."

Scanlon rolled his eyes, "Oh please, you're breaking my heart."

Scanlon tapped his Mobi and brought up a transit map. A Reclaimer-sized jump corridor extended from Banshee to Garron, then from Garron to Idris. Scanlon tagged a rapid set of commands, followed with his authorization code. The graphic overlay faded and he refocused his eyes on Jake.

"You're security cleared to Idris, two gate jumps will save you the gas." Then he added with a dour smile, "Don't say I never gave you nothin."

Scanlon walked into the airlock, one eye on the crate. He was happy as hell to get out of that stinking ship and whatever toxic waste sloshed around in the bottom of its oversized trash compactor. If his luck held out, he was ten minutes away from a hot shower and a stiff drink.

I GUESS IT'S TRUE WHAT THEY SAY

Incinerator 39, Brimstone

Doc gaped. *Just when I thought the day couldn't get any weirder.*

Heat poured out of the open incinerator. The big laser was off; this was just the heat that lingered inside the large ceramic-lined cylinder. An inscrutable slag of incinerate bubbled on the floor of the furnace, whatever residue that was capable of surviving a few hundred thousand degrees.

That part wasn't weird; hell, incinerators ran all the time in factory environments. Two guys at the back of a truck working a tailgate lift wasn't weird either. But when the load on the lift is a life-sized jade statue and the two guys are Petrovich and Charles Vane…   shit just got weird.

I cleared my throat and both men turned, frozen midway through wrangling the gloss green soldier towards the open door.

My eyes narrowed as I deadpanned, "I'd love to say I'm not surprised."

They looked at one another in silence. Petrovich shrugged, Vane spoke. "C'mon, give us a hand."

A rational man would have been tempted to turn and run. *I didn't see nuttin, I wasn't here.*

But my rational days seemed solidly behind me. This life, the crazy shit that goes on around here, has a way of sucking you in. I threw my shoulder against the back of a jade knee and heaved. We wobble-walked the statue the couple meters between truck and furnace, then pushed it through the open door.

"So somebody wanna tell me—" The sight of a green head in the air cut me off and I jumped to catch it before it hit me in the chest. The face in my hands stared up with sightless jade eyes.

"C'mon Doc, clock's ticking." Vane didn't have his usual growl, but there was an insistence in his voice. "This place is gonna be swarming with rent-a-cops and genius here didn't think to clean out the back room."

Petrovich winced, cussing under his breath in that odd linguistic blend of his.

I chucked the head into the furnace, then hustled to grab a series of broken parts off the back bumper. Based on the number of severed limbs piled like cordwood, somewhere were pieces of priceless history that looked like the *Venus di Milo*.

Petrovich grunted with a pair of ten litre buckets. I grabbed the next one that Vane handed down from the truck, groaning under the weight. The lable read DuroMAX Polycarbonate, with a color code for Yangtze River Green.

I looked up at Petrovich, who one-handed the bucket from my grasp and heaved it into the furnace. He pointed back towards the truck and shooshed me along with both hands. "Move faster."

Vane hopped down off the back of the truck, one bucket of jade-colored 3D printer substrate on each shoulder.

Probably half full, I muttered to myself.

Vane tossed a nod towards the front of the truck. "Front cab, paperwork, all of it goes."

I headed for the cab, suddenly aware that the dog had gone missing. I craned my head, looking left, right. Nothing. *She must be off taking a dump*, I muttered as I trotted up to the cab.

Yanking the door open I found an armfull of scanprints piled on the seats and floorboard. Photos of jade soldiers, some in the hold of a large freighter, some overlaid with photogrammetric grids. Designs for shipping containers, three-meter cubes capable of holding four statues in padded internal compartments. I walked back toward the furnace, flipping through sheets of blueprint.

"Sonovabitch Vane, you had Petrov 3D print a duplicate set of statues?"

That made no sense; even made from 3D scans they'd never pass up-close inspection. Then my breath caught in my throat and I looked up as I rounded the rear bumper.

"The ones on the news, the ones that got destroyed–"

I stopped, my eyes settled on Vane and Petrovich. They stood motionless, their own gaze focused to the left of the furnace.

"Yeah fuckstick, dey were fake." I knew that voice in an instant, even before he added "Clever Vane, real fuckin smart guy. So where ARE da real ones?"

My gut sank as I looked left where Lazlo stood in the shadows. It was just light enough to see that he had a large bore pistol in his hands. His beady little pig-like eyes burned at me. "I knew you two were in cahoots, I just didn't know how." He sneered in my direction, "So I followed you, and look where it leads me."

"I don't see where that does you much good." For a man with a gun pointed at his chest, Vane seemed not just unperturbed, but almost disinterested. "Every bounty hunter with cab fare is on his way here looking for you. How long you think you'll make it on the street; an hour, a day?"

Lazlo turned three shades of red. "That was your doing wasn't it?"

"No it was—-" I blurted the words before my brain could catch them. It couldn't have been Vane; the news said that Banu intelligence had traced communications back to a Brimstone-based organized crime figure who was believed to be behind the Co'Ral incident. There were very few things I would put past the reach of Charles Vane the pirate, but feeding info into a national intelligence service was beyond some pirate. That was…

I looked at Vane; there was no mistaking the smug look of victory. If my lips weren't sandpaper-dry I would have whistled, long and low. *Ho-lee shit.*

"Oh it was you Doc?" Lazlo must have taken my outburst as an aborted confession. "You and that schizophrenic freak you been 'pallin around with? You two been playin' footsies with the *tortugas* down in the Nek a whole lot lately. You set me up to be your fall guy?"

It was Vane's turn to look surprised. He flashed me a raised eyebrow that said 'We'll talk about this later.'

At the moment I wasn't sure there would be a later. Petrovich was sweating, maybe it was stress or just being stuck in front of the open furnace door, buckets of polycarb at his feet where he dropped them. Vane was just standing, although it struck me that he was edging ever so slowly towards the tail of the truck. Whatever his play, he'd need a diversion.

"Yeah, it was me you pint-sized sack of shit." The words tumbled out of my mouth with neither plan nor forethought. I thought Lazlo would pop a cork, eyes wide and mouth agape at a side of me he'd never seen. I just rolled with it.

"Do you have any idea how nauseating it has been to put up with your bullshit while we worked all this out? To have to explain things to you in tiny little words so they'd fit in that slug-brain of yours? Shit, Gort gets things faster than you do."

I watched Lazlo's jaw begin to tremble as his teeth ground together, saw the color flush across his face. His pupils went wide as rage filled his brain. There were other things going on, things I'd bet nobody else in earshot could imagine. Neurophysiological effects of stress that in a crisis rob you of awareness, of your ability to respond. Things that can stretch your reaction gap into seconds. If Vane moved suddenly, he'd have a huge head start.

I glared at Lazlo with an open hatred. *How do you like that science shit?*

But it wasn't Vane that moved first, it was a black and rust missile that slammed into Lazlo, shiny new teeth clamping on his extended arm. The gun fired once, the round whining off the pavement.

Lazlo screamed, thrashing against the weight of the dog that dragged brand-new fangs through the meat of his arm. Flesh tore in a spray of blood and the dog dropped to the ground.

Clutching the four fingers left on his mangled hand, Lazlo stepped back, his heel catching a bucket of polycarb. He stumbled, eyes wide with fear, and toppled backwards into the furnace.

Petrovich kicked the door shut and without a heartbeat's hesitation slapped the big red button on the panel. Blazing light poured through the smoked glass.

"God damn, Doc," Vane was the first to speak, his voice thick with amusement. "When you two decide to go, you're Hell on wheels."

I heard the words but barely processed their meaning, my focus on the dog. She stood looking at me, the strip of meat in her mouth ending with a severed pinky. Her tail wagged energetically, ears peaked up with pride. I rushed to her, hands sweeping across her sides in search of injury. There was none; the streaks of blood on her chest were Lazlo's last remains.

Vane took a knee next to the dog, running his hand through her fur in obvious admiration. Then he looked up, a thoughtful expression on his face as though something important suddenly crossed his mind.

"I guess its true what they say."

I shook my head. "What?"

He ruffled the dog and said with a laugh,

"Payback's a bitch."

EPILOG

Roxy's Place, Brimstone

The sign on the door read CLOSED.

Dead tired, Vane stopped in his tracks and looked at Doc, both men shrugging in unison. Roxy's place is never closed. With a 'what now' groan, Vane raised his fist and thumped it on the heavy metal door.

"Are you two idiots done stirring up trouble?" Though tinny over the intercom, the voice was clearly Roxy.

Vane looked left at Doc. "You done?"

Doc appeared thoughtful for a moment, then replied with a nod. "Yeah, pretty much."

Vane looked up at the camera, too exhausted to draw out the joke. "Open up Rox."

The only reply was the clack of electric bolts slugging back inside the door. Vane pushed and the two men walked in, dog in tow. They stopped just a few paces inside, eyes adjusting to the low light as the door banged shut behind them, bolts slamming back into place.

The saloon area looked like a tornado had run through it. Broken furniture, smashed mirrors, pieces of art showing off new bullet holes. The surge of alarm that hit Vane quickly subsided when he saw Roxy perched in her throne chair, drink in hand. A heavy caliber subgun lay on the armtable next to her, smoke slowly curling up from the muzzle. Spent brass and empty powercells were littered everywhere.

Roxy met the men with a withering gaze that she couldn't seem to maintain, breaking at last into a slow shake of her head.

"One thing you can say about this town," she offered with a sweeping gesture. "It's never dull."

Payback noticed the bodies first, sniffing her way along a blood trail to the corpses piled behind the Faro table. Nug was among them, a smoking cavity burned through his face. Thorvald sat next to him, still bleeding from a couple wounds but very much alive, drinking Johnnie Walker from the bottle.

Four of the corpses were pinks, decked out in various levels of body armor. More goddamn bounty hunters. One had a hole blown through his chest you could reach your arm through.

"Gort has a new toy." Roxy said before taking another long sip. "He was here talking to Ed when Benny the Twitch led these clowns to my door."

Doc looked up from the pile, concern evident on his face. "Ed? Is he OK?"

Roxy arched an eyebrow. "Is Ed OK?" She snorted, pointing at the pile with a measure of distaste. "Ed did most of… that."

Tangled as they were, damage to individuals in the pile wasn't immediately obvious. It took a longer look to realize that the blond-haired head staring face-up was attached to the body that lay face-down. Another looked to have the handle of a croupier's rake sticking out from his eye socket. It was a study in carnage wrought with on-hand objects.

Roxy's tone carried a droll note when she added "They caught him in one of his moods."

"Hey Doc." Vane spoke from across the room, pouring himself a drink behind the bar. He pointed at the floor where Benny the Twitch lay in a crumpled heap behind an overturned table. The line of bullet holes through the tabletop looked to match the ones that meandered down his throat, chest and hip.

Doc didn't shed a tear. *Much like payback, karma was a bitch as well.*

The irony struck a note and he looked around, then ambled back in the kitchen, rummaging for a couple minutes before coming out with a hefty raw T-bone. He waved the hunk of meat and said "Bill me" before tossing it to the tail-wagging dog. Payback trotted off to a quiet corner and began to munch noisily.

"So let's play 'How was your day," Roxy prompted. " I'm having a normal afternoon when these clowns come into town, along with a bunch of others, looking to serve a high-payoff warrant on Lazlo. Benny knows Gort is here, figures Lazlo must be upstairs. Things get unsavory, Ed goes unhinged and now he and Gort are hauling bodies out to the incinerator."

At the last word, Doc and Vane exchanged a fleeting glance like two schoolkids caught cheating.

"I saw that," Roxy scolded. "So let me guess, since Lazlo wasn't here and none of the off-world rent-a-cops can find him, am I safe to assume that Lazlo won't be surfacing any time soon?"

Doc answered with a taciturn expression. "It would take an act of God."

As if going down a checklist, Roxy turned her attention to Vane. "And you!" The pirate looked up from his beer, his real eye flashing wide. She pointed at one of the TVs on the wall where an INN newsfeed played, sound off. But the image showed a Merchantman disintegrating as it plummeted into a blue sun under the chyron TREASURES LOST.

"The news won't stop with this story of a crime that went all to hell; everybody dies, everybody loses."

Vane seemed to consider his drink for a moment before looking up, a 'cat ate the canary' grin on his face. "Well I wouldn't say that *everybody* lost."

Doc began to jump in with questions of his own when a Mobi rang and Vane triggered a response. "Yeah," he answered, holding a finger up for silence. "Yeah, real good. Come on home."

Vane dropped the call and fished a strip of holo from his vest. His grin may have been suppressed but his flesh and blood eye shined as bright as the prosthetic one as he rotated it to face Doc and Roxy. The amount of three-point-five million UEC gleamed beneath the words AVAILABLE BALANCE. He winked at Roxy and said "I think I can cover this mess."

"So how?" Doc asked. "I get that the statues on the TV were the fakes Petrov made, but where the hell did the real ones go?"

"I threw 'em in the trash," Vane muttered, dodging the wad of paper Roxy threw at him. "OK, well I threw them in a trash hauler, how about that?"

Doc's brow knit and he looked about, although it was clear his mind was elsewhere. "Son of a bitch," he muttered. "The designs for square shipping containers we just burned. That night in the rain…" He looked up, pieces coming together. "You put the statues in crates dressed up like cubes of compressed scrap metal."

Vane nodded, saying "Which Jake just delivered to Idris, as per our client's instructions." He let that sink in before adding. "The scrap you saw us shredding gave us the base cubes, and disposed of incriminating little items like the wings cut off an Avenger. Jake told me he could get 'em through the blockade, and it looks like he delivered."

"Pretty fucking brainy for a pirate." The voice came from the back of the bar where Ed and Gort lumbered in, splattered in blood. They dropped wearily into chairs.

Ed looked at Doc, waving at the remaining corpses. "I did my part, those are yours."

Before Doc could protest, Vane cut in. "Not so fast." His gaze snapped back and forth between Doc and Ed. "Since we're one little happy family airing our secrets here, what the hell is going on in the Nek?"

Doc froze like a deer in the headlights. He remembered Ed's warning about secrecy and given the conditions of the bodies on the floor, that threat seemed all the more tangible.

"Change of plans," Ed said to Doc with a backhanded motion, "we're gonna need their help." He turned and addressed the entire circle. "The Bomb wasn't a bomb, it was a test of a technology designed to open an artificial wormhole, something that you could just walk thru, drive through. Maybe big enough for ships, we don't know."

Ed looked around the circle, recognizing in every face the obvious question.

"Yeah, it's Vanduul. Leir makes perfect sense for a test. There is an existing natural wormhole from here to Vanguard so they'd have something to compare readings almost one for one. If it worked, really worked, they'da likely rolled in here and seized this sector to control both ends of their little science experiment. The rest of the galaxy would have taken it for a simple territory grab and nobody would have been the wiser."

Roxy was the first to respond. "So what happens now?"

Ed sighed. "The Xi'An are working it, they've been scratching at the problem since they got here but Doc came up with the key. We figured out how to open the door, on a very limited scale, which its pretty sure we caught the Vanduul by surprise."

"So why not open da fuckin door, toss in a nuke and shut it?" Gort offered the straight-line response. "Give those scaley fucks a taste of their own medicine."

"I'd love to," Ed chuffed, "but we have no idea what that would do. The rips left by the first event stretch a long way through this town. It could be bad. Egon Spengler sort of bad."

Looking at the blank stares, Ed realized that nobody got the ancient reference. He closed his eyes, accessed the EdBank and said "Uh, Try to imagine all life as you know it stopping instantaneously and every molecule in your body exploding at the speed of light."

Ed tried not to laugh when Gort thoughtfully responded with "That's bad."

"So you're gonna study it," Doc asked firmly, "figure out how to detect it, shut it down, stuff like that?"

"Precisely," Ed replied. "That's the plan anyway. The Xi'An don't trust anybody, UEE included, but they are working the problem jointly, positioned as an experimental theory they came up with. So nobody on the outside knows what we have in the basement. If they did, every government in the galaxy would fight to control it, even if just to keep it out of other hands. It would be chaos."

"So we just live here with this thing in the basement?" Vane spoke at last.

Ed shrugged. "Not much choice; transit restrictions are still in place; that isn't about to change. But keep in mind, this one didn't work, at least not the way it was intended. We don't think there's much chance of it stabilizing enough to hold open for more than a few seconds, but we're also pretty sure that the damage to the fabric of space makes this an unsuitable place for another detonation."

Ed sighed, the closed. "The big question is where will they try next, and you can be sure they will. The ability to open wormholes on demand, when and where you want, is a strategic game-changer. The Xi'An want to monitor this thing and will provide continued support to see this place keep operational. So for the forseeable future, we, all of us here, need to keep Brimstone running business as usual."

Ed leaned back "As improbable as it sounds, our motley group of pirates and thieves just ended up being the biggest secret on the front line of the war."

THE AFTER-THE-CREDITS SCENE

The Burn Ward, Sol System

"So that's when THIS crazy bastard says 'Fuck it' and stomps the gas!"

Laughter exploded around the bar as Amy snaked her way through the crowd, four cold mugs in her left hand and a platter of mixed drinks in the other.

The Burn Ward wasn't much different that a lot of other 'firefighter bars' around the 'verse. Portions were large and meaty, the jokes were off-color and the beer never stops flowing. The Ward wasn't strictly a firefighter joint, the regulars included cops, paramedics, nurses, pretty much anyone involved with the thankless, bloody business of saving lives.

The walls of the Ward were a museum to that battle, where pictures of the saved hung alonside memorials of the lost. Patches, ball caps, decals, PASS devices; almost anything with a unit ID or service designation littered every shelf and mantle. Between it all a junkyard of odd parts was nailed to the wall, bits and bobs picked up from the floor of the ER or from 'the back of the bus' as paramedics refer to the business end of an ambulance. Every piece, a life saved.

"No wait, wait," Casey motioned the crowd to silence. A slender imp who radiated energy, Casey was his happiest at the center of attention, grinning ear to ear, cocky as a rooster. But he did tell a damn good story. As he reclaimed center stage, the room settled down to the low ramble of TVs and clatter from the kitchen.

"So I'm thinkin," he jumped right back in, "there's no way in hell we're gonna make it in time, right? We're staged back with fleet, maybe a couple thousand kilometers out, and that lifepod is falling straight into the big blue star. So what does he do?"

Casey let the question hang for just a second, milking the anticipation. "He mother-fuckin TAC-Jumps that bitch!" Casey slapped his mug down on the table for dramatic emphasis, foam sloshing across the table.

More roars, mixed with the occasional coughing "Bullshit!" from the peanut gallery. Casey snapped around. "Say what? Bullshit? Bullshit?? Hey Major, and I telling this right?"

All eyes turned to the four figures in black UEE flight jackets. The patches on their shoulders depicted dark angels with flaming wings plummeting out of the sky. It wasn't often the Ward hosted regular military, much less ace fighter jocks. Today was special.

The one called Lucifer raised his hand, shaking his head. "I was there, I can swear to it. Damn near ripped my canopy off." Amid the 'oooohs' from the crowd, Casey took a strutting victory lap.

Amy leaned across the table to plunk down several drinks and whispered in Dugie's ear. "What's a TAC-Jump?"

Dugie leaned in close, speaking over the catcalls. "Jump drives are made to cover a long distance really, really fast, but you ease in and out of 'em. A tactical jump is, well, sorta crazy. You spool up the jump drive with no end-point set then shut it off the instant you start to jump. You end up covering a relatively short distance in a blink, but you come out of it going way, way faster than a boat should go."

"That sounds dangerous."

Dugie gave her a dead-flat look. "Suicidal. Worse when you do it facing a star."

"There it is, there it is! Turn it up!!" Casey barked over the crowd, pointing madly at the TV on the wall. He grabbed the remote from a fumbling patron and spun the volume to 'really fucking loud.'

"- INN has received exclusive footage of the incident." The broadcaster ran color commentary over video captured by one of the many drone-cams chucked out by the Sabers at the onset of battle. The EMP had just hit so the scene felt oddly slow compared to most of the combat footage coming in off the Vanduul line. The sweeping, pointed nose of a big dark ship stuck into the frame from far left, with a handful of fighters tumbling around it. Engines sputtered, lights flickered.

Casey added his own overlay. "Wait for it, wait for it… BOOM!"

A brilliant flash burst on the screen, seemingly meters above a stalled Saber. It looked like an invisible cannon just fired a large red projectile. Casey whipped his hand at the screen and literally screamed "That's my boy!!!"

The red blur streaked across the scene so fast the camera had trouble following and focusing at the same time. It framed the object, a bright red Cutlass, hurtling towards the immense blue disk of the pulsar star. The paramedic vehicle went into a sick sliding drift, every engine and thruster spewing flame into the direction of travel. A panel ripped away from the forward port canard.

The crowd roared its frustration when the image on the TV froze, the remote still in Casey's hand.

"Hold up, hold up," he chided like a carnival barker. "Check this out." He hopped up on a chair and pressed his fingertip on the screen. "See… THAT little black dot?" He waited for the nods. "That's the pod."

More shouts, cheers mixed with the odd "No way!!"

Casey cocked an eyebrow. "Oh yes-fuckin'-Way bitches, check this shit out." With a click the video leaped back into motion.

The Cutless started coming out of its slide, still tracking about fifteen degrees off line-of-travel when incandescent blue streamers started appearing along its forward edge. "Corona contact bitches," Casey chided, stabbing a finger at the screen. "He is scraping noses with a motherfuckin' star."

Amy set down her platter and watched. She was no pilot but you didn't need to be to see that the red ship was hanging way over the edge. The cheers, whistles and OMGs continued as the Cutlass thundered after the lifepod, racing its descent into fiery oblivion. Like the Cutlass, the pod trailed whisps of burning blue.

For a moment it looked like the two would collide and Amy found herself holding her breath.

Light, like some powerful searchlight, shot out of the belly of the Cutless, sweeping across the pod. The ship thundered past but the beam seemed to stick, to stretch like a radiant rubber band. The nose of the Cutlass rose, engines blazing at full as the ship struggled to climb against the star's immense gravity.

Amy understood enough about tractor beams to realize that at that moment, the pod was a boat anchor. For long seconds it looked like gravity would win the fight. The fins on the Cutless sagged, the entire airframe shook. A light bar tore away.

Then the pod shifted upwards, the elastic band snapping back. Engines screaming, the Cutlass skipped off the outermost curve of the star and hurtled into the black.

Amid shouts, cheers and high-fives, Casey dropped into his seat, exhausted with the telling. "Oh my god" he muttered, shaking his head. "Oh my god, that is the shit."

Somebody clicked off the TV and forks rapped against glass as Lucifer stood, his own glass in hand. Three of the Fallen stood up around him. A fifth seat sat empty, a full glass on the table.

Lucifer looked around the room, shrugged, then raised his glass.

"There's a few things you know as a fighter pilot, one of them is that not everybody makes it home. But we know... every door-kicker, trigger-puller and pipe-hitting motherfucker on the line knows... that we aren't out there alone. We fight the enemy, be it Vanduul, pirates, whatever." He paused, making eye contact with the emergency responders gathered around the room. "But you guys fight Death. You go out there and grab the Old Man by the throat and tear our shot-up, on-fire, dead-in-space asses out of his grip."

Around the room eyes glistened wet, muttered 'amens' mixed with an assortment of oorahs and hooahs.

"We started that fight as a team of five, and —"

"Hey, what'd I miss?" Fumbling with his zipper Danny Stone, Fallen Three, hustled to his seat and snatched up his glass. He looked at Lucifer's dead stare and shrugged "What? I had to pee."

Lucifer shook his head, put an arm around Danny's neck and continued. "And thanks to you, five of us came home. Here's to you."

A cloud of glasses lofted into the air, all tipped in one direction.

Gunza, captain of the EMS rescue ship *Valkyrie*, stood in the corner, silent throughout. He was a bear of a guy; tall, broad shoulders. The shot glass of very old MacCallum looked tiny in his hand.

He seemed uncomfortable with the attention and fixed his eyes on the smokey liquid, inhaling the scent before raising the glass to the room in return and throwing it back.

Wincing from the liquid fire he looked up at last, a grin parting the heavy beard before he shrugged and said, "Nobody dies on my watch."

Printed in Great Britain
by Amazon

37802702R00136